THE DEADWOOD STAGE

His name was Andy Lord and he drove one of the Deadwood stages. He was the best driver the company had, and until he encountered a U.S. Deputy Marshal named Jeff Lavender it had not occurred to him to do anything but drive stages. But that changed suddenly, dramatically, and for some men, fatally, in one wild afternoon and evening when he and Marshal Lavender rode south to an immigrant settlement named Grasshopper. He still had no idea of the full implication of what he had become involved in, and until the last shot was fired and he got back up to Deadwood, no one told him. When they did, he could hardly believe the story.

D1738292

THE DEADWOOD STAGE

John Kilgore

A Lythway Book

CHIVERS PRESS
BATH

First published in Great Britain 1987
by
Robert Hale Limited
This Large Print edition published by
Chivers Press
by arrangement with
Robert Hale Limited
1991

ISBN 0 7451 1436 9

British Library Cataloguing in Publication Data available

THE DEADWOOD STAGE

CHAPTER ONE

SPRINGTIME

It was unlike the stagecoaches used on heavily travelled routes. It was not even the dull, functional colour of those large vehicles, the ones that require a six-horse hitch even on level ground.

It lacked the storage capacity in the rear boot or beneath the driver's high seat of those heavier stages, and while it could accommodate four passengers facing one another, two on one seat, two on the opposite seat, it was customary for stations to sell seats for six people, which added to the discomfort of knees striking the knees of the people facing one another, not to mention arms, shoulders and thighs rubbing.

If one or more of the passengers happened to be women the results of that crowding were quite often acute embarrassment.

There was usually not much conversation. For one thing the Deadwood stage had leather thoroughbrace springs which made the rig sway back and forth as the larger stages also did, but it also swayed slightly from side to side. If the roadbed was washboardy, as it ordinarily was after springtime freshets had flowed across it, and summer heat had baked the ridges into

1

permanent fixtures, the stage's moving motion was a combination of both pitching and swaying.

'Sea sickness' was not unusual among passengers. Even those to whom this kind of travel was no novelty and who were unlikely to have to suddenly and fiercely push their heads out the open upper part of the doors to vomit—a not-uncommon occurrence even on the larger stages.

There was also reticence; in the part of the country where the Deadwood Stage Company operated, and excluding the occasional uninhibited drunk, almost everyone who travelled was a stranger.

Towns were far apart. There were way-stations, usually at intervals of roughly fifteen to twenty miles, depending upon whether the roadbed was fairly level, or tilted and mountainous. They had been established less for the convenience of passengers than for the horses; these were usually changed at each way-station.

The stations were isolated. For that reason keeping the people to operate them, horse-handlers, possibly a blacksmith, a man or woman to have meals cooked when the coaches were to arrive, was a constant headache for the company. Not infrequently men who agreed to hire on as way-station employees had personal reasons for needing jobs that provided them with seclusion. Some were fugitives, some were fleeing other aspects of former lives, and it was common to find that the horse-handlers were hard-drinking individuals.

The ideal situation was for the company to sell someone a way-station franchise. That way they would be more likely to stay through the fiece winters and the blast-furnace summers. They had a vested interest in running their stations profitably. The trouble was that it was hard to sell those franchises, and since the company had to have people out there at those isolated places they hired whoever came down the road in need of employment, or, as Andrew Lord, the most tenured among the coach drivers said, Charley Kinnon who owned the company and whose corralyard and office was in the town of Deadwood, closed his eyes when he hired people for the way-stations.

A few years back he had tried to hire former soldiers. That had been when Indian raiders had been around to sneak in and cut out all the horses and run them off, usually just short of sunup. If the horses were stolen in the night it was thought the thieves had not been redskins since Indians preferred not to risk being killed by a stray bullet in the darkness. It had something to do with a prevailing redskin conviction that those who were killed in the darkness had to spend Eternity stumbling around in darkness.

3

This was not always the case. Charley Kinnon had lost horses to raiders from the south border country, redskins who had no such beliefs.

Andy Lord had been around in those days too. Although he was a spare, ruddy-complexioned man with pale blue eyes, a mouth like a bear-trap which was partially concealed by a droopy dragoon moustache, his weathering had worked in reverse; Andy did not look as old as he was. Nor did he act as old, although within reason age in an active, rawboned, spare man who had never had a sick day in his life, and whose parents had lived to very advanced ages, was likely to have a very high tolerance.

Andy knew the Deadwood Company's 'runs'; at one time or another he had tooled stages over every one of them; had in fact pioneered a few of them. And he knew the Mandan Hills to the north, as well as the far-distant Big Sleep Mountains to the south. He had trapped and hunted all this country, even some of the grassland cattle country between the mountains. Andy had lived in Deadwood for eleven years. Before that it was anyone's guess what he had done or where he had come from, but one thing had been abundantly clear to Charley Kinnon the day he hired Andy—on a relief basis to substitute for another driver who had become ill—Lord could handle horses and coaches.

In eleven years he'd had six coaches stopped and robbed without loss of life, and he'd successfully kept three runaways from overturning at high speed and perhaps killing passengers. Andy was a calm, quiet, seasoned individual who rarely inaugurated a conversation. He lived in the company bunkhouse at the rear of the corralyard in Deadwood, along with constantly departing and freshly-hired hostlers and other drivers. He was a private individual but people liked him. He and Deadwood's town marshal Lewis Brant, who showed a faint trace of Indian blood, were two of a kind, in build, in reticence, in hard-headed practicality and also in their dry, sometimes sly variety of humour. They had been sitting in on Thursday night poker sessions at the Deadwood Saloon for six years, rarely missing a night summer or winter. That was something else they shared, a fondness for poker.

In a community of shifting goals and residents, Andy and Lew Brant were regarded as fixtures. Deadwood had a relatively stationary percentage of inhabitants, mostly those who owned businesses or who, as with Andy, worked for someone else whose business was permanent, but by far the greater percentage of Deadwood's people came and went, either seeking work in an area where hiring was seasonal and therefore unlikely to

5

offer much, even during the riding period on the cow outfits, which was roughly from March through September, or had come west cherishing a dream of settlement, and that too was full of discouragements. If the bleak winters did not freeze those people out, summer droughts would, or, if a winter had been mild and summer rains arrived, harassment, sometimes night-burnings, otherwise contempt in the towns and frank disapproval on the ranges would take its toll.

Mostly, the cow outfits did not have to resort to harassment. They were established, firmly rooted in their countryside. They could afford to simply wait; the Deadwood country looked like it would be good for crops, but it wasn't. Topsoil was in many places no more than three inches deep, deep enough to support flourishing grass, but much too shallow for row-crops; turnips, potatoes, beets, corn, squash, the staple of homesteaders for whom there were rarely markets in the cow towns where they could sell their surplus anyway. There was a name for this kind of waiting. It was called 'starve-out', and with some settlers it took longer than with others, but almost invariably whether those people hung on for one season or three, perhaps four seasons, they would load their wagons with pots, pans, a bedstead or two, a ramshackle table and chairs, maybe a little iron cook-stove, a herd of runny-nosed children, and head out.

Marshal Brant's primary obligation to the community was policing Deadwood, which he did competently, but since the entire area was unincorporated even though it had been surveyed into townships, there was no county seat, which meant no county law enforcement. No one cared; in fact very few people understood that the jurisdiction of town marshals ended at township lines. When there was a difficulty town marshals were commonly summoned and they acted in the capacity of county law officers even though, technically, they did not have that kind of authority.

Marshal Brant, for example, had been called into the far countryside many times to hunt rustlers, horse thieves, trouble-makers of many kinds, and he invariably functioned as a law officer should, which was all people really cared about. The technicalities would take care of themselves in time, but when there was trouble people were disinclined to wait for townships to become counties, which would have county sheriffs.

One thing that had not made Lew Brant many friends was his roughshod policy of going after stockmen or their riders who harassed settlers. In his defence Lew had stated many times that law enforcement as he understood it could not be based upon personal feeling. Nevertheless, there were ranchers who did not approve of Lew Brant. They said he was partial to settlers.

But the raids had been diminishing the past few years, since it had dawned upon the cowmen that they did not have to resort to night-riding, they could achieve their ends by just going on about their business and allowing attrition to thin out the settlers.

However, what people called 'progress' but which was actually 'growth', got to the point where for every settler family that loaded up and went back wherever they came from, at least one newly-arrived wagon of emigrants took their place, and in fact, while no one had any idea what the actual statistic was, it had to be more nearly like three arrivals for each departure. As Lew told Andy Lord one Thursday night in the heated Deadwood Saloon with a bottle between them and the cards favouring neither one of them, on several of Lew's rides up toward the highlands for about a year now, he had noticed more smoke from chimneys than he had ever noticed before, and furthermore if his rides were at intervals of several months, the smoke rising above settler shacks or wagon-camps was visible from places where there had been no smoke, no buildings, not even any wagon-camps only a couple of months earlier.

Andy sipped whisky, studied his cards, tossed down three, drew replacements, re-studied his hand and disinterestedly said, 'Yeah. I've noticed it too. More strangers riding the stages. Not just drummers and travellers, sometimes emigrant families with kids and boxes of personal stuff. Homesteaders full of questions.'

Andy raised pale blue eyes in an absolutely expressionless face. 'I call.'

Lew had to pause long enough to review his cards, then smiled a little. 'Call and raise two dollars,' he said.

Andy peered at the cards again balancing his decision. 'Call and raise another two dollars,' he stated.

Lew stared across the table from eyes that were nearly black. Then he abruptly tossed in his cards face down. One thing he had learned about Andy Lord. He never bluffed.

He hadn't been bluffing this time, he spread the cards face up. He had a full house, a pair of red eights and three kings.

Lew grinned ruefully and reached to refill his glass. It was almost too warm in the saloon, and while the big old room was two-thirds full there was not a lot of noise except when a late springtime fierce little wind came scrabbling round the eaves or capriciously caused a powerful down-draught that made the cannon heater exude grey smoke from every room. Then there was coughing and cursing. But as a rule the smoke dissipated quickly.

Andy was dealing when Marshal Brant said, 'Did you know Charley Kinnon sent a big freight wagon down to Rock Gate?'

Andy shook his head as he arranged his cards. 'No. Why? Some freighters break down?'

'No. Some settlers did. Two wagonloads of them travelling together,' replied the town marshal, discarding two cards and waiting for their replacements. 'All I know is what one of your yardmen told me. The settlers had a camp in the trees on the west bank of the river at Rock Gate. Like gypsies. They been down there for some weeks. You know how that goes; they did laundry in the river, aired things out, rested their horses...'

'Why did Charley send 'em a wagon, Lew?'

Marshal Brant replied from behind his poker hand. 'They lost their horses.'

Andy cocked an eyebrow. 'How ... lost 'em?'

'I got no idea, Andy. That's what the yardmen told me. They lost their livestock, was marooned down there, one of them walked all the way to Deadwood and paid Charley cash in advance to send a big outfit down so's they can transfer their belongings and come up to town to set up camp somewhere while the menfolk look for the horses.' Lew studied his friend's face then said, 'You got openers?'

Andy shook his head. 'No. You?'

Brant's reply was to toss his cards down.

10

Andy dealt out another hand.

CHAPTER TWO

A MORNING RUN

Andy went south with one of the sturdy Deadwood coaches. They were all painted a uniform colour: Yellow running gear, a sort of coppery light red above. He had four passengers and some light freight in the boot. He had four horses on the pole—it was flat country to the terminus of his run southward near a settler community called for some unknown reason, 'Grasshopper'.

The way-station was a half mile north of the village and there was not much association back and forth. Andy left town an hour ahead of sunrise and was passing the tree-lined bank of the Blue River near Rock Gate crossing when he saw breakfast smoke rising down along the riverbank. He looked for a wagon-camp and not only found it but also saw the big freight wagon Charley Kinnon had sent down to those people.

Andy's interest was perfunctory. He would not even have known anything was wrong if he hadn't played poker with Lew Brant the previous night. He did not think it particularly unusual for the yardman who had tooled the big

11

wagon down there yesterday, to still be there with the wagon this morning.

His hitch was in a long lope. Within seconds he was past the place of considerable smoke with open country on ahead all the way down to the Grasshopper way-station.

Andy was bundled into his knee-length old wool-lined blanketcoat. His hands and wrists were protected from the morning cold by smoke-tanned gauntlets. The sky was flawless, cold-looking with dying stars; his passengers, two couples with a small child, had the flaps down to keep the cold out, and his horses were road-wise, knew where they were going and established their own measured gait to get down there. About all Andy had to do was watch for deep chuckholes in the road, keep the horses lined out straight, and watch the new day get born.

He did not smoke nor chew, which made him something of an oddity among stage drivers, nor was he a hard drinker. Even during the bitterly cold winters with temperatures down as low as thirty degrees below zero, when he stamped in out of the snow to stand by a stove until the horses were changed, he might drink one cup of hot laced coffee, but that was all. Andy Lord had come up in a hard environment. By the time he could have learned a lot of range-country vices he was too old to care about developing them.

This particular morning when he braked to a halt because one of the horses had somehow got astraddle a trace, one of the passengers climbed stiffly out, walked forward to watch Andy free the tug, get it back on the outside where it belonged, then re-hitch and he offered Andy a pony bottle of brandy. Andy smilingly declined. The passenger shrugged beefy shoulders, tipped his head and swallowed a couple of times before putting up the bottle as he said, 'What's the next stop?'

'Grasshopper. About seven miles down the road.'

The passenger regarded Andy quizzically. 'Grasshopper . . . ?'

'Yeah. I got no idea why it's called that.'

'How big is it?'

'Kind of small,' Andy replied, moving back toward the near front wheel-hub which was used as a step up. 'It's one of those settler villages you run across now and then. Around it folks try farming.'

The passenger nodded, tightened the muffler at his throat and walked back to climb inside. Andy listened for the sound of the door latch, then kicked off the binders and whistled up his horses.

The sun came. It brought instantaneous brilliance but no warmth. That would be along in another couple of hours. This was early springtime, winter never yielded gracefully in

13

the plateau country.

About two miles north of the Grasshopper way-station Andy saw three riders herding a band of what looked like mules and horses almost due west. He squinted to make out details but even the glass-clear air and the sun-bright brilliance of this flawless, chill morning could not make up for the distance. He could not even be sure there were mules among the horses. The reason he thought there was, was because mules travelled differently from horses, especially at a lope, which was the gait those animals were being held to by their drivers.

By the time the newday heat was arriving they were down at the Grasshopper way-station, which was being operated this year by a gorilla-like older man and his expressionless Crow woman. The man's name was Ezra Kamp, he had small eyes that nearly disappeared when he smiled or laughed. He was a good hand with livestock and his woman was a fair cook of ordinary meals.

Andy assumed Ezra Kamp was making money. He rarely fed beef, and otherwise deer meat and antelope cost no more than the time required to find them, the bullet to kill them, and the labour to prepare and cook them.

When the passengers went inside to soak up more warmth Andy remained outside where Ezra's two strapping barrel-built sons were

14

taking horses off the pole to be led around back to corrals while a fresh hitch was brought forth to be harnessed and backed onto the tongue for the return run.

Ezra stuffed a foul little pipe, got up a head of smoke and said, 'How is Charley?'

Andy was removing his gauntlets. 'Fine. You know Charley—like a kitten in a box of shavings even when there's not much to do.'

Ezra smiled, his eyes got lost in the heavy flesh of his cheeks, and he removed the little pipe to expectorate before speaking again. His little eyes were upon the untidy scattering of warped buildings down the road a little farther and upon the east side of it. He poked in that direction with the little pipe. 'Not like last year, Andy. There's wagons of them folks arrivin' over there two, three times a week.'

Andy gazed down there. Smoke was rising above the clutter of shapeless structures. Someone down there was working steel over an anvil. A few of Grasshopper's inhabitants had already worked the soil up for plantings. 'Thrifty place,' he said dryly. He had been over there three or four times, mostly out of curiosity but also once or twice to deliver light freight.

Ezra Kamp spat again then bit down on the stem of the little pipe. His gaze was narrow and hard. 'They'll take over the land,' he said gruffly. 'Like crickets, won't be long before you

15

won't be able to turn over a stone without findin' them or their offspring under it.'

Andy finished this discussion with a nod at the way-station man and turned. 'Business good is it, Ezra?'

'Too early to tell yet, but we're hopin' there'll be a lot of travel this summer.'

Andy closed that topic too. It was one of those perfunctory things a man was expected to say and he had said it. 'On the way down I saw someone drivin' what looked like a fair-sized band of horses and maybe some mules.'

Ezra's shrewd little half-hidden eyes came up. 'Where?'

Andy gestured. 'West. They were movin' right along. Too far for me to be able to make out much.'

Ezra puffed small bursts of smoke for a moment, his eyes again fixed on the Grasshopper community. He said, 'Andy, I ain't usually one to run off at the mouth ... there's somethin' goin' on down there.'

The driver turned and also gazed across the road southward.

'Goin' on, Ezra?'

'Well ... livestock goin' through down there, comin' in at night sometimes, bein' corralled by lantern-light, then bein' drove out maybe a little before daylight the next morning.' Kamp again removed his little pipe to expectorate. He did not raise his eyes to the taller man's face when

16

he resumed speaking. 'It's been goin' on for several weeks now, since the snow went off the mountains to the south.'

Andy drew the reasonable conclusion to such an announcement but watched smoke above rooftops at the settler-village, and listened to the high, musical ring of metal being shaped over an anvil, without speaking. A man wanted to be very careful about voicing such ideas.

Ezra waved with his little pipe, but before he could pursue the topic his pair of massively muscled, dour looking, dark sons led the fresh hitch out and Andy went over to lend a hand getting them on the pole. As he was doing this Ezra came over and said, 'The Wellington stage from the south should have been here by now to take your passengers on over the mountains.' Ezra made this announcement in an even tone of voice, but he also wagged his head as though annoyed.

One of the Indian-looking younger men raised up to look at his father. 'They're never on time, Paw.'

Andy listened to this exchange without much interest. The people who had the franchise to operate Wellington Freight & Passenger company out of the town of Wellington some sixty miles south, had a reputation for being slip-shod. They'd had that kind of reputation since Andy had been in the country.

He finished with the traces and moved ahead

17

to buckle straps to the singletrees and to the tongue with Ezra following. The gorilla-built man knocked dottle from his pipe against a boot-heel, pocketed the pipe and watched Andy work for a moment before he said, 'Maybe the marshal might want to ride down and visit over at the settlement, Andy.'

The horses were ready. One of the burly younger men was standing at the head of the leaders. The other younger man went back around the side of the log building and did not return.

Andy smiled at Ezra Kamp. 'All right. I'll tell him what you said . . . You got anything to go back?'

Ezra nodded. 'Yeah. I expect my other boy went back to get it. Looks like a shipment of dry goods for the store up at Deadwood.' He called to the younger man at the head of the leaders. 'Ambrose, go help your brother fetch them boxes around here so's Mister Lord won't be delayed.'

When they were alone Ezra shuffled back toward the boot in order to be handy at helping his sons load the freight as he said, 'I ain't by nature a suspicious man, Andy. On the other hand I don't need to get hit in the head with a rock to know it'll hurt.'

Andy walked back and leaned on the near-side big rear wheel. 'Are you talking about the livestock comin' and goin' down there?'

'Yes. An' if you tell Charley, you can also tell him me'n my boys been keepin' a night-watch on the company animals in our corrals. No point in him worryin' any more than he already does.'

Kamp's two sons came around the side of the log main-building, each of them carrying a large crate. Andy started ahead to help but Ezra stopped him. 'They ain't heavy, they just look heavy, and since they're addressed to the general store up at Deadwood, we figured they was probably full of bolt goods or somethin' like that.'

Andy watched the younger men load their crates in the boot and walk briskly back the way they had come. He asked Ezra how many crates there were, and the squat gorilla-like man replied shortly, 'Four. If you want the boys can put the other two up in the forward boot.'

That is what was done. To more evenly distribute the weight. Andy helped them this time. Ezra had been correct. Despite the size of the boxes, they were lighter than they should have been.

He thanked the boys, pumped Ezra's massive paw, and with one of the boys back in front of the leaders Andy swarmed up to his seat, evened-up the lines, eased off the binders and with a light flip of the lines started his fresh hitch moving.

The burly man and his sons watched as Andy

cut a wide turn that carried him off the packed roadway on to softer ground before he could line out his hitch northward up the centre of the main roadway. Andy waved, the Kamps waved back then sauntered in the direction of their main-structure where those passengers were warm, finally, and had eaten. The morning was passing. Along with its drift toward afternoon the heat built up until Andy had to lean to shuck his coat.

He made excellent time on the return trip. For one thing he was carrying less weight. For another thing he no longer had to avoid all the chuckholes.

He ate cold meat from a saddlebag he always took with him, chewed on raisins and washed it all down from an old dented canteen.

He reflected upon what Ezra Kamp had hinted at, and decided there were perhaps as many logical reasons for settlement-people to be active with livestock this time of year as there were reasons for suspecting them of being involved in crimes, and wondered if Lew Brant would be in town when he got back up there after nightfall.

He had manifests in his pocket covering those big wooden crates he was carrying, and once, when he let the hitch slog along at a steady walk for a couple of miles, he pulled out the papers and tried to decipher someone's unbelievably bad handwriting, gave it up and returned the papers to his pocket. He didn't really care about what was in the boxes anyway.

By mid-afternoon the heat was almost as bad as it would be a couple of months hence, at the peak of summer. The sky was faded, pale blue without clouds in any direction. The sun seemed scarcely to be moving.

He had no passengers and although he did have a schedule he made no attempt to hold to it. Whether he arrived in the darkness at seven o'clock or eleven o'clock, would make very little difference; what he particularly did not like doing was pushing horses in fierce heat even when he had passengers.

CHAPTER THREE

DIVERGENT TRAILS

When Andy turned up into the corralyard hostlers arrived with lanterns to take over. He climbed down, pulled off his gauntlets and looked for Charley Kinnon. One of the yardmen said Charley had left about an hour earlier. Andy went back to the bunkhouse to scrub, then headed for the cafe.

Because it was late he was the only customer and although the fat cafeman was usually garrulous, for some reason he had very little to

21

say tonight, which suited Andy Lord who was hungry and a little tired.

After eating he wandered up to the saloon, saw Charley Kinnon sitting alone with a bottle and glass at a distant table, got a glass from the barman and walked over. Charley looked up, smiled and gestured. As Andy sat down Charley shoved his bottle forward. 'How did it go?' he asked.

Andy was filling his little jolt-glass when he replied, 'Like it usually does. Brought back four boxes for the general store.' Andy downed his shot of whisky, pushed the glass aside and glanced around the room. 'You seen Lew Brant this evening, Charley?'

Kinnon shook his head without taking his eyes off Lord. 'Nope. Not since about mid-afternoon. Something wrong?'

Andy's reply was slow. 'No, most likely not.' A sixth sense made him change the subject. 'Ezra Kamp sent you his best wishes. Seems the Wellington stages don't keep very good schedules down there.'

Kinnon nodded. 'Yeah. There is nothing new about that, is there?'

Andy shrugged. Kinnon sat studying the taller man. He volunteered information about the freight rig he had sent down to Rock Gate to help those stranded emigrants, then he also said, 'The outfit had to lie over because the settler-men were scouring the countryside for

22

their livestock; weren't around to help load the rig with their belongings.'

Andy nodded. He had seen no activity at the settler-camp early that morning. 'Did they get back?'

'Yeah, in mid-afternoon. The people loaded their belongings and came up to Deadwood. They got a camp along the river a mile or so north—up where that clearing is the freighters used years ago.'

'What about their livestock?'

'Not a trace except for tracks,' replied Kinnon. 'I think that's where Lew went today—to figure out if those animals wandered off. A lot of times when emigrants get around a town they get careless about things like that.'

Andy had one more drink with Kinnon then returned to the roadway where a chill was setting in. Down the road a short ways and up on its opposite side there was a light showing through the barred window in the jailhouse front wall. He went down there.

Lew Brant looked up from his desk where he had been sitting soaking up the wood-stove heat. His hair was awry, his hat was lying atop papers on an untidy desk, and Lew nodded without smiling as he gestured Andy to a chair. 'Cold,' he said impersonally, eyeing his visitor.

Andy ignored the mention of the weather. 'Were you out lookin' for the livestock of those settlers down at Rock Gate?'

23

'Yeah.'

'Driven off, Lew?'

'Yeah.'

'South?'

Brant tilted his chair forward and planted thick arms atop his desk as he replied, 'Due south. Maybe three, four men behind them.'

Andy launched into a recitation of what Ezra Kamp had said down at the Grasshopper way-station and Lew Brant's very dark eyes did not leave Lord's throughout. Finally, he settled back off the desk again and said, 'I didn't go that far. I didn't get down to the settler camp by the river until mid-afternoon. It was turnin' dark and gettin' cold by the time I'd figured out what had happened. You can't track much in the dark so I came back ... You had supper, Andy?'

'Yeah. About an hour ago. You?'

Marshal Brant slowly moved his head up and down. Andy's impression was that Brant had something on his mind that he probably preferred not to talk about, so Andy leaned to arise from the chair as he said, 'Well; just wanted to pass along what Ezra Kamp said about that settler-village down yonder.'

Lew came out of his reverie and quietly said, 'Sit down, Andy.' He then made a motion toward the stove. 'There's hot coffee in the pot if you want any.'

Andy did not leave the chair.

24

Marshal Brant arose and paced over near the gun-rack on the office's rear wall, turned with his back to the weapons and said, 'Andy, it's not just those emigrants. While you been out on your runs lately, I been gettin' complaints from stockmen as far north as the foothill ranges.'

'Losing livestock?'

'Yes.'

Andy regarded the dark-eyed man in silence. Brant went to the stove, filled a crockery cup with black java and returned to his desk. As he sat down he said, 'I've done some riding. Been askin' around. I'll tell you one thing. If it's those sodbusters down yonder, they're a hell of a lot smarter than any sodbusters I ever ran across ... I tracked three bands of driven livestock. The tracks petered out a couple of miles from where the animals were rustled.' Lew's eyes puckered as he regarded his friend. 'Sometimes when people brush out sign, they got to leave their own. Not these people. They leave nothing. So if they're everyday homesteaders they're a right unusual bunch.'

Andy said, 'If you want to go down there, Lew, I'll ride along.'

Brant smiled for the first time, a warm, amiable smile. 'I know you would, Andy. But what I'm up against isn't just ridin' down to the Grasshopper settlement and asking around, because right now whoever is doin' this stealin' don't seem to be worryin' much. My badge down there would change that—if those folks are involved.'

'What do you want to do?'

Marshal Brant hooked powerful arms behind his head and gazed at the ceiling as he replied. 'Play In'ian. Scout 'em up down there at night. Maybe lie out a mile or so and watch for a day or two.' Brant came forward again and leaned on the desk. 'What your way-station rep told you fits in with the fact that those rustlers always head south . . . Andy, you got any idea how much livestock's turned up missing lately?'

'Nope.'

'Well, neither does anyone else, but from what I've had to listen to from the people who've been raided, it's a hell of a lot, and I doubt if most of the cowmen really know the extent of it yet; they don't go counting horns very often except maybe at gatherin' or markin' time. What I was sittin' here thinking about when you came in, is that when folks figure out how much they really have lost, if I haven't come up with something in the meantime, they're goin' to ride me out of Deadwood on a rail.'

Andy finally went after a cup of hot coffee, took it back to the chair, sat down and held the cup without raising it as he studied the town marshal. He'd had no idea anything of this magnitude was going on. But then he probably would not have known; he was a whip, a

26

stage-driver; he was rarely in town more than a day and a night, what gossip he heard around town or at the saloon had to do with old feuds, alliances between wives or husbands whose spouses did not suspect infidelity, the usual gossip for any small town.

He finally tasted the coffee. It was not bad. He drank it half down and scowled at the cup as he lowered it. Livestock theft was ordinarily something that everyone heard about very early on. Irate stockmen were never reticent about something like that.

Lew Brant had been watching Andy Lord's face. He chuckled as he said, 'Don't feel bad. Lots of folks around here don't know what's goin' on. The reason? Andy, I asked the stockmen not to talk about it.'

With a shove Andy put his coffee cup upon the edge of the marshal's untidy desk. 'You'd have a reason, eh?'

Brant's earlier amusement became an ironic and humourless grin. 'Yeah. I know this much from figuring. Serious rustling, this kind of stealing, hasn't ever been a problem in the area until early this spring ... And maybe those folks down at Grasshopper got a hand in it, but a settler ridin' around the countryside, especially now when stockmen are fillin' out their work crews for the upcomin' season an' there are riders all over the range, would be seen. The feelin' the way it is, he'd be run off—at the very least. At the worst someone would overhaul him a little ... Andy, my point is this: No one rustles livestock off the top of their head. They study herds, ranches, the routines of rangemen, they lie somewhere for maybe two, three days, then—when they've got it all figured out—they ride in at night, make their gather and run for it ... Andy, I made a point of askin' in each case of a raid if anyone saw any strangers, maybe emigrants, on their ranges before they was raided ... They hadn't. Not even once.'

Lord considered reaching for his cup before the java got cold, but instead he cocked back the chair waiting for Marshal Brant to finish what he had been leading up to.

'They're not just ridin' in the dark and takin' a chance on finding the best horses and cattle. They already know those things before they make a raid.' Marshal Brant paused, perhaps for effect, then he also said, 'Think about it. They aren't raidin' blind and they aren't scoutin' up herds—then how in the hell do they know where to raid, and how to get away with it?'

Andy finally did retrieve his coffee cup and drain it. He replaced it on the corner of the desk and cocked back his chair again. 'Tell me,' he said. 'An informer among the ranchers?'

Lew Brant was silent for a long time before saying, 'Maybe. That's what I figure to start on next week. Find out which riders weren't on the ranch a night or two before the raids.' Brant leaned on the desk eyeing his friend. 'But it don't have to be a rangeman, Andy. It could be anyone who can move over the ranges without anyone wondering about him bein' out there.'

Lord thought about that. There were a number of people such as the town medical practitioner, Doctor Brady, or someone from the general store, even from the trading barn at the lower end of town, even Marshal Brant himself, who could ride anywhere without arousing much interest or suspicion.

When he left the jailhouse office a little later Andy walked slowly toward the corralyard and its bunkhouse wondering if perhaps Lew Brant wasn't creating something that did not exist; an organised livestock-stealing conspiracy? He'd heard tales of such things but in all his years in livestock country he had never encountered any such thing.

As he paced through the dark, quiet yard in the direction of a solitary lighted window along the palisaded rear wall where the bunkhouse stood, it also crossed his mind that if as much livestock had been rustled as Brant had hinted at, why then, hell's bells, it sure could be such a conspiracy, even though from his knowledge of such things, horsestealing and cattle rustling were usually accomplished on a somewhat hit-or-miss basis by one or two riders. At the

29

most, perhaps four or five riders.

From what Brant had said Andy had got the impression that the present situation was anything but trivial. He bedded down with his problem and awakened with it the following morning before sunrise. Later, as he was crossing the yard toward the dark roadway and the cafe with its steamy window and orange lamplight, Charley Kinnon hailed him from the rear door of the roadside office.

Andy veered over in that direction. Charley pointed toward the wood-stove and its coffee pot as he said, 'I got a schedule for you to dead-head west to Finchville, pick up six passengers and some mail sacks, and return.'

Andy drank bad coffee eyeing his employer. Finchville was forty miles west of Deadwood. Round trip he would be on the road for about eight hours. If the lie-over at Finchville was an hour—it usually took longer to get loaded and wait until fresh horses were put on the coach—he would be lucky to return to Deadwood before nightfall.

'Six passengers and mail sacks,' he repeated, draining the cup and sinking it into a bucket of greasy water beside the stove.

Kinnon nodded. 'And two small crates for us. Horse hardware I ordered from Denver a couple of months ago.'

Andy nodded, re-buttoned his old coat which he had opened inside the office because the room was unusually hot, and went to the roadway door as he said, 'How much time do I have?'

'Half hour. I'm goin' back there now to get the yardmen to stir their stumps. Plenty of time for breakfast, Andy.'

Lord closed the door after himself, braced into the cold and trudged down to the cafe. Ordinarily Charley Kinnon knew at least a day in advance when he'd have to schedule a trip. But not always. Occasionally unexpected events arose and Andy assumed that that was what had happened this time. He rarely questioned Charley.

At the cafe the local medical man was hunched around a platter of breakfast steak, biscuits and gravy. No one else was in the cafe. As Andy sat down the doctor turned his head. Andy said, 'Morning, Howard.'

The physician, whose name was Howard Brady, nodded and returned to his meal. By the time Andy's breakfast had arrived the doctor was leaning back stuffing shag into his pipe. He'd had two cups of black coffee along with his meal and now his earlier dourness seemed to have vanished. He lighted up, puffed smoke and watched Lord eat for a moment before he spoke. 'I don't think the Lord figured we should be up and around before daylight, Andy, otherwise he'd have made us so's we could see in the dark.'

Lord grunted, chewed, and nodded his head, but after he'd swallowed he glanced around. This was the first time he could remember ever having seen the medical man abroad before daylight. 'Deliverin' babies?' he asked.

Doctor Brady puffed a moment before replying. 'No. Not this time. There's some settlers up at the old freighter camp alongside the river. Someone ran off their horses and mules a day or so ago.'

Andy stopped chewing. Horses *and mules*?

'. . . One of them came down with something yesterday and of course they waited until midnight to come for me. I just got back.'

'What did he come down with?' Andy asked, and the medical practitioner pulled thoughtfully on his pipe before answering.

'I'm not sure yet. Symptons are like pneumonia but those same symptoms go with a half dozen other ailments. Anyway, he's got to stay abed, be kept warm, and tomorrow I'll drive back out there.'

Andy nodded and returned to his meal. This was about the time people came down with respiratory ailments; a whole range of ailments for that matter. Andy nodded as Doctor Brady arose to depart.

Later, as he was also finishing his meal Marshal Brant walked in. He glanced around at the empty room, nodded at Andy and seated himself beside him. He gave the cafeman his

32

order, waited for him to depart, then leaned and said, 'I'm goin' down there today. Want to get away from town before anyone sees which way I rode.'

Andy stared. 'You think there is someone here in Deadwood who's tangled up with livestock thieves?'

Lew blew out a big breath before replying. 'No. Not necessarily, but in case I'm wrong I'd as soon not have moccasin telegraph warn anyone at the Grasshopper settlement I rode southward.' Brant eyed Andy. 'You got an early run?'

'Yeah. Drive over empty to Finchville, pick up six passengers, some mail sacks and whatnot, and return.'

Marshal Brant's breakfast arrived. He attacked it. Nothing more was said between the stager and the lawman. Andy was back across the road at the corralyard as the last trace was hitched to a singletree. Charley Kinnon himself opened the gate. As they passed one another Charley said, 'Take your time,' and the driver called back as he always did when Kinnon said that, 'Sure.'

CHAPTER FOUR

THE RETURN TO DEADWOOD

Andy Lord's arrival at Finchville was just a little short of the rising heat so he was still wearing his old blanketcoat as he climbed down in the centre of the Finchville corralyard. The company rep over there had three Mexican yardmen. They seemed to have been expecting Lord's vehicle because they had a fresh four-up harnessed and waiting at a rack.

Andy entered the rep's office, nodded at two women and two men in city attire who were waiting there in office-warmth, then the rep offered Andy hot coffee, which he accepted and stood with his back to the stove while the passengers got ready to board his stage for the run back to Deadwood. They did not have much luggage so there was plenty of room atop the stage and in the boot for mail sacks and several small wooden boxes which were loaded while Andy waited inside with his coffee.

The Finchville company representative came to the door and said, 'Everything is ready, Andy.'

Lord had expected to eat in Finchville. Ordinarily he would have had plenty of time because the harness horses would not have been standing in their harness when he arrived.

But he had driven greater distances on even less than a cup of coffee so as he passed the rep on his way to the forewheel of the coach he nodded without complaining.

When he made the wide, closely calculated turn from the corralyard into the roadway, barely grazing duckboards on the turn, he raised a gauntleted arm in acknowledgement of the salute from one of the Mexican hostlers, lined out his hitch and kept it at a steady walk for a half hour, until the horses had all been warmed out, then whistled them up into an easy lope. It was about one o'clock in the afternoon, there was heat and as a consequence of that there was also dust, but as long as the coach rocketed ahead the trailing dust banner could not overtake it, also, by the time Andy was ready to enter one of the lay-bys where there was a spring-fed stone trough where the horses could tank up, he had been walking the horses for a mile and the dust did not cause complaints. Andy knew his trade. Being a stage-driver, like being a genuine horseman, required a lot more knowledge than just sitting up there looking impressive.

At the turn-out while he was watering the horses the pair of city men strolled up. One of them was much older than his companion. They seemed not only to know one another but to be travelling together—presumably with

35

their wives.

The older man smiled as he admired the condition of the horses. Andy was accustomed to this, for a fact Charley Kinnon kept good animals. The younger man asked if Andy knew where there was a settlement known as Grasshopper. Andy eyed the younger man thoughtfully for a moment before nodding. Neither of his male passengers looked or dressed like people who would have business in a thrown-together, hard-scrabble settler village.

'It's about half a day's stage ride south from Deadwood,' he said, folding the collapsible buckets to be stowed under his seat in the front boot now that all the horses had been watered.

The older man had been watching Andy. He continued to watch him as he put the buckets away and turned back to face the men. He was finished and ready to roll again, but he was also polite.

The old man, who was grey and lined with a shrewd pair of small pale eyes, looked affable as he asked a question. 'Is there a way-station down there?'

Andy had a boot up the wheel-hub as he replied. 'Yes. About a half mile north of the village. It's run by a feller named Ezra Kamp. You folks ready to go?'

The men nodded, got back inside and when Andy heard the door latch he swung away from the trough, got lined out again on the roadbed and as usual allowed his animals plenty of time to get set before he eased them over into a gallop.

Andy was not by nature an inquisitive individual but this afternoon he was; at least to the extent of trying to imagine what business his male passengers were engaged in, and why they would want to go down to that squalid settlement on the south roadway.

He had not arrived at a conclusion by the time he saw dust rolling up upon itself to the south. There was nothing else of interest to watch, so he tried to see what was out front of the brown banner. It would not be cattle; no rangeman in his right mind would push cattle that fast and that hard. It could be horses, they would travel like that without effort, but he could not be sure what it was. The distance was considerable, perhaps as much as three or four miles.

The dust was rising in the wake of something travelling southward. Andy's course for Deadwood was due easterly. Within minutes he was too far ahead to watch the banner without turning on his seat, which he did not do.

He had Deadwood in sight while the sun was still over his left shoulder. This would not have happened if those horses had not been waiting when he'd arrived at the Finchville corralyard. Neither would it have happened if he'd had time for a leisurely meal.

37

He anticipated an early supper, maybe a scrubbing down in the bath-house out behind the tonsorial parlour where a chunk of brown soap and a fresh towel cost two-bits.

He was reflecting on Marshal Brant's situation as he made the wide curve where the westerly roadway intersected the north-south stage road. Deadwood was less than two miles onward, there was still heat, Andy slackened his animals to a slogging walk so that they would arrive dry and breathing easily at the corralyard, otherwise they could not be watered, something which never seemed to concern passengers but that unfailingly concerned drivers, yardmen, and ultimately company officials.

The percentage of whips that had been fired by stage company authorities for whatever reasons, was highest among the drivers who brought hot, winded horses in off a run.

Andy gauged the turn into the corralyard as he had been doing for years, got his leaders within inches of the off-side plankwalk, and eased them around in a sort of sideways cake-walk until he could sight between their ears past both gate posts to the centre of the corralyard.

He made it handily. Several old gaffers sitting indolently in warm afternoon sunlight on a bench in front of the saddle and harness works, cackled with appreciation. Andy threw them a smile then eased back on the lines, looped them around the brake-handle and went down hand over hand to the ground.

Charley Kinnon was standing in shade near the rear doorway of his office. He was wearing one of those green celluloid eye-shades seen most commonly among railroad telegraphers. He said nothing. In fact as Andy paused to pull off his gauntlets Charley walked past him to the four passengers, introduced himself and shoved out a pale hand.

Andy did not feel slighted, he felt hungry.

At the cafe the proprietor was sipping sarsaparilla and mopping sweat off his fat neck with a limp blue bandana. He waited until Andy was seated to stow the bandana and put aside his sarsaparilla. He was a large-boned man which made his obesity less noticeable, but he was fat. He was also soft as putty, though there were signs that once, years earlier, he had been a burly, powerful individual. He said, 'Didn't expect you until after dark.'

Andy nodded. He hadn't expected to be sitting here until after dark either. 'Too early for supper?' he asked, knowing he wasn't.

'No. No, I been simmerin' things for a while. You got a choice, Andy. Antelope roast or beef brisket steeped in corn brine. Me, I'd take the corned beef.'

Andy nodded. 'Corned beef, coffee, whatever you got under the pan on the pie-table...'

39

'Too bad about the marshal, ain't it?' the cafeman said casually.

Andy did not move except to raise his eyes. 'What about the marshal?'

'Hell,' the cafeman exclaimed disgustedly. 'I forgot you wasn't in town today ... He got shot.'

Andy let his breath out slowly. 'Lew Brant got shot?'

'Yeah. He's over at Doc Brady's place, but the fellers who brought him in ... Hey; don't you want to wait for the corned beef?'

The passengers he had brought to town earlier were walking in the direction of the roominghouse when Andy went past them taking thrusting strides. They watched with lively eyes as he turned in at a picket fence in front of a cottage where no one appeared to have cut weeds for a long time. They probably saw Doctor Brady's hanging sign over the front porch.

Andy did not knock, he lifted the latch and pushed the door inward with some force. Doc Brady's front room, which served as a reception area but which had also served as a working area enough times when emergencies had arrived there, smelled powerfully of disinfectant.

This afternoon the smell was less noticeable because a front window was open onto the roadway. The reception area was empty. Andy

40

paused, there was a dingy hallway to his right, to his left were several closed doors. He had never visited Doctor Brady's place before.

The decision of how to proceed was solved for him by the appearance of Howard Brady in a greyish cotton coat reaching nearly to his knees. As they gazed at one another the doctor said, 'Something wrong, Andy, or are you here because of Marshal Brant?'

'Marshal Brant, Howard. What happened—how is he?'

The doctor crossed to a chair without haste, seated himself and motioned his guest to be seated but Andy remained standing. The doctor drew a very large white handkerchief from one of the pockets of his grey coat and proceeded to roll it between his palms as though drying them. 'He's dead, Andy,' the medical practitioner said quietly, not raising his eyes, perhaps because he preferred not to see any more shocked faces today.

Andy sat down. 'Dead,' he repeated softly, not as a question but as a statement.

The doctor finally looked at his visitor. 'As for how it happened—I don't really know. About two hours ago some folks travelling through in a private coach found him lying beside the road a few miles north of the Grasshopper way-station. He was alive when they tried to make him comfortable inside their rig ... I don't see how he could have been but

41

they swore that he was breathing when they picked him up. Regardless of that, by the time they got him up here to me he was dead.'

'How—what killed him, Howard?'

Doctor Brady stopped rolling the handkerchief and made as though to stand up. 'Do you want to see him, Andy?'

'Howard, what killed him?'

'Four bullets. Either carbine or rifle bullets. I was taking them out when I heard the front door open as you arrived. Tomorrow I'll be able to tell you which weapon they came from—but right now I'd make a guess that they were rifle bullets, and that they hit him from a considerable distance. They did not go through and they did not break any bones ... I'd figure from that they were fired at him from distance ... They hit him in the back; any one of them would have put him down but I think only two of them would have killed him outright. All this is pretty much guesswork right now, Andy.' The doctor got to his feet. 'Care to come see?'

Andy stood up holding his hat in both hands. 'No,' he said and walked back out where the air did not smell of disinfectant.

He went down to the corralyard and turned in. Charley Kinnon and two yardmen saw his face. Only Kinnon spoke to him. 'Is it true he's dead, Andy?'

'Yeah. What the hell happened, Charley?'

No one knew, not the stage company man,

not the barman across the road where news usually arrived early, not anyone that Andy encountered during the rest of the day. Down at the livery barn he was told that no one had brought Lew's horse and outfit in.

He walked out behind the livery barn to lean on a cribbed corral pole and stare unseeingly at the confined horses.

Andy Lord was one of those men who valued a good friendship as though it were a kinship.

The shock of how he had learned of the killing had something to do with his present numbness, his limbo state of existence. He'd had no real opinion that for Lew to go down south and scout up that settler village could be dangerous. Certainly not dangerous enough for anyone to be shot to death.

Four bullets in the back!

CHAPTER FIVE

A STRANGER

Charley Kinnon told Andy to take the next day off, to go down along the river fishing, or maybe take a slow ride through the springtime wild flowers up toward the foothills.

Instead he got his Winchester from the roominghouse, buckled his shellbelt into place, took a company saddle animal and rode south.

He heard one of the Deadwood stages coming long before he saw it and went off the road eastward, which was what he'd had in mind anyway. When the coach whirled past the driver raised a gauntleted hand and Andy waved back. The driver was a younger man, some kind of kin of Charley Kinnon's, otherwise at his age and with his lack of experience he would not have been given the responsibility of driving.

The sun was high and visibility was excellent when Andy found a set of shod-horse marks pointing southward from the direction of Deadwood. He crossed them looking farther east for more sign. He did not believe Lew Brant would have ridden this close to the roadway, but evidently Brant had. Andy had to turn back and sashay until he picked up the tracks again. Of course if Lew had approached the settlement after nightfall it would not have made much difference whether he was close in or farther out.

Except that evidently it had made a difference.

Andy came up out of a broad, shallow arroyo and halted to watch a pair of riders loping westward. They were barred from his sight as they sped past the way-station where the coach that had passed him was sitting out front with the tongue on the ground. When they merged

44

into view again they were still holding their animals to that mile-eating lope. They had probably come from the settlement.

He remained on Brant's tracks until they went down into another and deeper arroyo. Here Lew had followed the gully southward, presumably so as not to be seen. Andy rode beside the tracks until the arroyo floor began to tip upwards. Fifty or so yards ahead the arroyo merged with higher ground near a jumble of ancient dark rocks covered with what looked like pock marks. And here Lew Brant's trail ended.

Andy swung off, tied the horse and quartered very slowly working out the itinerary of the shod-horse marks of which there were quite a few.

Here, Lew had dismounted. Perhaps to watch the settlement from the only place of concealment around. Grasshopper was no more than a mile and a half onward.

Andy found boot-prints and painstakingly searched until he found more. It looked to be either three or four sets of prints made by different sized boots, all of them run over and evidently badly worn.

The tracks he thought had belonged to Lew Brant were near a shoulder-high big old scabrous rock. This was where Lew had stood while spying on the settler-village.

Since he had come out here alone, in the

darkness, those other footprint-marks must have been made by someone who came down here into the rocks, probably after Lew had been shot.

Andy tipped down his hat and leaned against the massive rock looking back the way he had come, and elsewhere. No one was as good a shot as Doc Brady believed these men had been for a very basic reason. At rifle-distance in the night it would be impossible to see a man let alone hit him. Nevertheless Doc's premise was solidly based. Rifle bullets that did not go through someone were probably spent, as Doc thought. From a shorter distance they would not only pass through a man but they would leave an existing hole a man could press three fingers into.

As Andy leaned in thought putting some scraps into place, it occurred to him that if he could locate that place from which those men had killed Lew Brant, he might get lucky and also find out something about them as men, as individual killers who might have been hired to kill Lew on sight and were hurrying toward Raton Pass to reach sanctuary in southern Colorado by now or, just as likely, they were down the far side of the southward mountains on their way to Mexico.

Unless of course they had been sentries watching the northward flow of country, and were not hired killers at all but were perhaps

46

inhabitants of the settlement. Andy was inclined to believe the latter theory because even if those had been hired gunmen, and had either caught sight of Brant or heard him in the night, unless they had been hired specifically to kill the marshal the chances were excellent that they would not have bothered with a lone rider in the darkness; someone they would not be able to recognise because of darkness.

Andy got back astride, made a slow search for sign of anyone close by, saw no one and started quartering again, this time looking for horse-tracks approaching the rocks. He found them, but eastward a half mile and they stopped over there while several sets of boot-prints went toward the rocks. Where the boot-prints stopped was close enough to where Lew had been standing that carbines would have done the job, and even then the slugs would have passed through Brant's body since Doc had said none of them had flattened against bone.

He dismounted walking back and forth studying boot-prints and hoping to find an ejected shell casing. The prints were clear enough but there were no brass casings. He halted, spat, wagged his head over the fact that Lew Brant's murderers had paused after the shooting to pick up all their spent casings before walking over to examine the man they had shot. Whoever they were, they were methodical, probably experienced, and

47

cool-headed killers.

He stood a while in sunlight gazing southward toward the settlement. There were little drifts of chimney smoke lying veil-like above the huddle of rude structures. He watched for movement down there while speculating about why the killers had hauled Lew a couple of miles northward to be left beside the road where those people in the private rig had found him.

It was almost as though they wanted him to be found.

A half mile eastward someone astride a sorrel horse came up out of an arroyo. Andy caught movement in that direction from the corner of his eye and turned.

The arroyo ran all the way down behind the settlement. He speculated that the rider of the sorrel horse had seen him from the settlement, and had approached him from the settlement using the depth of the arroyo for concealment.

He stood relaxed, hands hooked in his shellbelt watching the rider approach. It was a tall, lean man whose face was half-shadowed by the pulled-forward brim of a sweat-stained old brown hat. The man had a carbine under his right saddle fender and was wearing an ivory-stock sixgun around his middle. He looked intently at Andy as he approached him, and when about thirty yards separated them the man stopped, leaned on his saddlehorn, spat

48

amber then said, 'You lose something, mister?'

Andy had a better view of the stranger's face when they were closer. It had coarse, bony features, a slit of a mouth and the eyes were set deeply beneath a craggy overhang of forehead-bone.

Andy answered in the same flat tone the stranger's question had been asked. 'No, I didn't lose anything—just a good friend is all. He was shot last night over in those rocks.'

The lanky man chewed, expectorated amber again, resumed his chewing and studied the man on the ground. 'Well,' he said, 'there was gunfire out here somewhere last night. Woke me out of a sound sleep.' The lanky man swung to the ground and led his horse with him as he walked a little closer. 'Who was this friend of yours?'

'The town marshal of Deadwood.'

The lanky man with the shrewd, deeply set eyes chewed for a moment or two, then said, 'Is that a fact? A lawman. You sure about this?'

'I'm sure.'

'And this lawman—how bad off is he?'

'He's dead,' stated Andy: waited a moment then said, 'Who are you?'

The lanky man ignored the question to ask one of his own. 'Are you takin' the marshal's place; you got a badge, mister?'

'No. I told you, he was a friend of mine.'

The lanky man nodded slowly over that.

'Friends mean a lot,' he said quietly, almost as though making this statement to himself. Then he also said, 'What was he doin' out here last night?'

Andy had answered the last question he was going to answer for the lanky man. 'What are you doin' out here?' he said.

The stranger considered Andy's expression for a moment and evidently decided Andy's mood was not friendly because he forced a little apologetic smile as he answered. 'Saw you from the settlement. Watched you walkin' around lookin' at the ground, got curious and rode out.'

'What's your name?'

'Bert Wales. What's yours?'

'Andy Lord.'

Bert Wales stood in thought for a long time, chewing and gazing in the direction of the rocks where Lew Brant had been shot. Eventually he said, 'I'm new around here. Come up from the border country. Just arrived in Grasshopper a couple of days ago.' The shrewd, sunk-set eyes came slowly back to Andy. Bert Wales seemed to have more to say but he did not say it, he simply stood studying Andy Lord for a long time, then shrugged and turned to mount his horse.

Without even a nod Bert Wales went back to the arroyo, down into it and disappeared.

Andy mounted, returned to the rocks,

watched shiny blue-tail flies swarming over signs of blood, then started back toward Deadwood. He hadn't come up with much but the farther he rode and the more baffled he became while trying to find answers to what he knew, the more it appeared to him that what Lew had inadvertently done, perhaps, was pick a night to go down toward the settler-village when something was going on, and the men who had shot Lew had not been waiting for him, they had probably been out there waiting for something else. It would not require four armed men to kill one unsuspecting man, but it would take four riders to pick up a swiftly-moving gather of stolen horses and keep them moving out of the country.

By the time he reached Deadwood the sun was sinking, stove-fires were scattering smoke-fragrance over the town, and Charley Kinnon was still at his office when Andy returned the company horse. Charley looked quizzically at his driver when Andy entered the office from out back. Charley did not bother to pretend he did not have an idea what Andy had been doing. He said, 'Find anything?'

'Found the rocks where Lew was standing when they shot him, and the place they shot him from. Four of them.'

'Did you go over and talk to Ezra Kamp?'

Andy had not even thought about the raffish way-station manager. 'No. But some feller rode

51

up from the settlement on a big sorrel horse and we talked for a while. He asked questions an' I answered them. That's about all there was to it.'

'What was his name?' Kinnon asked.

'Bert Wales. He said he'd just come up from the border country. Hadn't been in the settlement for more than a couple of days.'

'What else did he say?'

'Nothing. When I quit answering questions he rode away.'

'Did he know anything about the shooting?'

'Only that it woke him up.'

Charley leaned so far back the chair squeaked. 'Doc's finished. We're goin' to bury Lew tomorrow.' Charley continued to lean far back gazing at his driver. 'The Town Council's lookin' for someone to serve out what's left of Lew's term as marshal. As far as I know now, they haven't had any luck. I don't think I'd want to put on the badge of a man who'd just been bushwhacked to death. Andy, what the hell was Lew doin' down there last night in the dark?'

Lord was on his feet near the door, he returned his employer's gaze and shrugged powerful shoulders then walked out into the late evening on his way over to the cafe.

Doc Brady was eating alone at the cafe counter when Andy walked in. Both Doc and the cafeman looked up to see who had arrived.

The cafeman nodded but Doctor Brady simply went back to his meal.

Andy went over, dropped down beside Brady, told the cafeman he'd eat whatever was handy providing it was dead, and turned toward Brady as the cafeman shuffled off to his cooking area.

'You finish the examination?' he asked.

Doc went right on eating as he bobbed his head up and down, sucked his teeth briefly then said, 'It came out about as I figured it would, as I told you last night.' Brady's eyes came around slowly to Andy's face. 'With one exception. The bullets.'

'What about them.'

'Did I tell you they were rifle slugs?'

'You said you thought they were. Were they?'

'Yes, but where I was wrong was in figuring rifle bullets would be spent by the time they hit Lew, so while they could cause his death and not exit the body . . . Tell me something, Andy. Did you find the place where the bushwhackers fired from?'

'Yeah.'

'How far would you say it was from where Lew got hit?'

'Not very far, Howard. Maybe one hundred yards give or take a few yards.'

Doctor Brady slowly smiled. 'They were rifle slugs. I've extracted enough in my time to be unshakable in that conviction.'

'Howard, rifle bullets from one hundred yards would have torn holes in Lew.'

Brady continued to beam. 'Ordinarily, yes, but I'll tell you something about three of those bullets; each one of them had more than one set of clinch marks where the casing had been crimped. I have no idea why all four gunmen reloaded their own casings and cut them back each time so that by the time they were firing at Lew the casings did not hold even as much powder as a carbine bullet. That is the answer to why rifle bullets at about one hundred yards did not go plumb through Lew and emerge still moving on his far side.'

Andy leaned back as the cafeman placed a meal before him. As before he waited for the cafeman to return to his cooking area before addressing Doctor Brady again. 'What about the fourth bullet, Howard?'

'Only one crimp scar but I suspect its casing had been cut back for reloading many times too, otherwise as we both know it would have gone through Lew and most likely no one would ever have found it.'

As he had been speaking Doctor Brady had also been reaching for his coffee cup. His plate was clean, he had finished supper but appeared in no hurry to depart. He said, 'There is talk around town of appointing a new marshal.'

'Who?'

'As far as I know no particular name has been mentioned ... How about you, Andy? I'm still on the council. If you want the job I'll sure put your name up for consideration.'

'Howard, I'm a stager.'

'Lew's job might pay better, Andy.'

'I doubt it, Howard. No thanks, don't bother to put my name up in nomination.'

But Brady had grown increasingly fond of his idea since mentioning it. 'You'd be good at the job,' he said persuasively. 'I can't think of anyone I'd rather see wearing Lew's badge.'

Lord finished his meal, drained the coffee cup, arose and lightly slapped Howard Brady on the shoulder as he headed for the door. 'No. Plain and simply no, Howard ... Good night.'

CHAPTER SIX

A MOURNFUL MAN

Without a lawman to take his woes to an old rancher from the eastern range country beyond Deadwood ended up at the saloon loudly complaining about the lack of legal protection at the only moment he'd needed it in ten years. Some low-down, measly, night-riding sons of bitches had run off his remuda of working horses after they had been segregated in a small

55

meadow for the use of his riders who, the very next day, were to begin gathering cattle.

This garrulous announcement caused some head-shaking and a few comments about other raids around the countryside lately. One of Charley Kinnon's hostlers was in the saloon when this all took place and went back to the corralyard to tell his employer. He also told Andy Lord, who was in the bunkhouse killing time until evening when he was slated to take a Deadwood coach south to the Grasshopper way-station.

Andy listened, said nothing, and after the yardman left he sank into an old rickety chair with his thoughts. Later, he hiked over to the saloon but the exasperated rancher was gone. The barman knew who he was and gave Andy his name, but there was no way that Andy could have ridden as far as the cowman's yard and gotten back in time to take a stagecoach south to Kamp's way-station.

He went moodily back to the bunkhouse. They had buried Lew Brant earlier in the day; the entire town had turned out along with some stockmen who had been in town, and who'd had no idea Marshal Brant was dead.

Andy made a fresh pot of coffee, took a mug of it out back to the big holding corral with him, and leaned there watching horses and mules while slanting sunshine warmed his back.

A suspicious man, he told himself, would

56

arrive at the conclusion that those four riders who had shot Lew late at night out on the range, had not been waiting for someone to shoot, they had been waiting for horsethieves on breathless horses to bring a stolen band down where the four fresh horses and men would take over.

Lew had just chosen a very bad night to go skulking around the Grasshopper settlement area.

He reflected on that band of horses he had seen a few days earlier, with what he was sure were mules among them, being driven west below the way-station at a fast pace, in broad daylight.

He also dredged up the things Ezra Kamp had hinted at. He finished the coffee, returned to the bunkhouse to rinse the cup and re-hang it from a nail over his wall-bunk, then he began to prepare for the southward run. Charley Kinnon came back to the bunkhouse with a pony bottle of brandy which he put on the table when he said, 'Take it with you. Keeps a man's bones from aching and clears his head.'

Andy looked from the bottle to his employer's face. Charley knew Andy rarely drank. He smiled and said, 'Thanks,' then went back to getting bundled up. The sun was gone but daylight lingered. Charley said, 'I put one of those little wooden crates you brought back from Finchville in the boot. You can deliver it

57

to Kamp. It's some new JIC bits he wanted.'

Andy nodded again and picked up his smoke-tanned gauntlets, ready to drive. As they were moving across the yard side by side Charley looked up. 'I don't know what anyone can do, Andy. We all liked him. I guess a man just has to let things like that wear themselves out.'

The yardmen had his coach about ready. A gangling, awkward youth with a lard bucket full of heavy black grease and a paddle for applying it, had finished with all four wheels. One of the yardmen was now going around giving the backward-turning big lug bolt a couple of final twists.

Andy looked toward the office, then elsewhere before he asked a yardman if there would be passengers. The man nodded. 'One gent. He's at the cafe. Was over there anyway—here he comes now.'

The passenger was a man as tall as Andy Lord and slightly stooped. He had a scraggly moustache and hair that curled down the back of his neck from beneath his stiff-brimmed hat. Andy, who had been doing this for years, guessed his passenger was a cattle buyer.

As he was examining the harnessing before climbing to the high seat Charley came over and said, 'There'll be freight from Wellington for you to haul back from Kamp's station but as far as I know, no passengers ... I'll be waitin' when you arrive. Good trip, Andy.'

The slightly stooped, almost mournful-looking tall man strolled over, hands in pockets, stood examining the coach then climbed in without a word or a nod to Andy and closed the door.

Out of town there was a little summer breeze along the ground. It swirled dust ahead of the coach, even ahead of the four horses, but it never let the dust rise high enough to bother anyone. There was a fairly large moon; it was lopsided but its brightness would help later, after full darkness arrived, and although it was not yet cold Andy was wearing his blanketcoat because he would not want to stop a few hours down the road to put it on.

He drew up at a lay-by to water the hitch. The mournful-looking man climbed down to lend a hand. He did not seem to be very talkative and Andy had not been in a talkative mood all day and part of yesterday, so they worked mostly in silence, but when the buckets had been stowed the tall, mournful-looking man said, 'You make this run often, do you?'

Andy nodded. 'Often enough to know every rock in the road by its first name.'

'You know folks down in Grasshopper, do you?'

Andy considered the tall, unsmiling man. 'Not a damned soul, mister. You can walk over there from the way-station but I've seldom had any reason to go over there.'

The stooped man fished forth a cut plug and offered it. Andy declined because he did not chew. In fact he did not even smoke an occasional cigar. The passenger gnawed at a corner of his plug, pocketed it, spat then said, 'Sure sorry about your local lawman.'

Andy nodded, waiting for the passenger to walk back and climb into the coach, but he made no such move. He shoved big hands into trouser pockets, chewed and eyed Andy Lord. 'You made this run a lot of times over the years, eh?'

'Yep. Every week for about six years. Sometimes three or four times a week.'

'Then you know the country.'

Andy said nothing. He was beginning to have an odd feeling about the mournful-looking man.

The tobacco-chewer seemed rooted in place. If Andy had been on a tight schedule he'd have been annoyed, as it was he was beginning to try to figure the tall man out. He looked like a fairly successful stockman, maybe a cow rancher.

The passenger finished studying Andy and said, 'I never been in this area of the country before. I been a hell of a lot of other places, but not down here. I'll tell you what that means to me, driver. I don't know anyone and can't trust anyone. You understand?'

Andy's brows dropped a notch in a faint

troubled scowl. 'Not exactly,' he responded.

The mournful-looking man pulled one hand from a trouser pocket. Even by watery starshine and moonlight Andy had no difficulty recognising that small badge with a star in the centre and a circular ring all around it with the legend 'U.S. Marshal'.

Andy's breath ran out slowly as his eyes lifted again to the other man's face. 'Lavender,' the mournful-looking man said. 'It's a flower and a scent and it's also my name. Jeff Lavender.'

Andy nodded forgetting to state his own name. It turned out not to be necessary. 'You'll be Andy Lord.' Lavender spat then smiled a little at Andy's expression. 'Like I told you I don't know anyone down here, but one of the other lawmen working out of Denver knew a feller in Deadwood named Brady. Howard Brady, the pill-roller.'

Andy leaned back against the coach beginning to see where all this was leading. 'Friend of mine,' he told the federal lawman.

Lavender smiled and inclined his head. 'Yes he is. He told me I could trust you with my life. Now I never go that far trustin' anyone, but Mister Lord, I'll tell you why I'm holdin' you up right now ... Stolen horses, mules and cattle. They've been traced by their brands to this area. They've been showin' up as far north as Montana along with some forged bills of sale.' Lavender paused to spray amber again.

'We got some real pitiful letters from some settlers who got a wagon-camp north of Deadwood. We been turning up their animals in tradin' barns and other places, along with a lot of other stolen animals. We been impounding them wherever we found them, but that's not what we are after—we know where most of those critters came from you see, and right now I want to know who has been sellin' them to traders.' Jeff Lavender paused, looking steadily at Andy Lord. 'The reason I'm explaining all this to you is because of what Doctor Brady told me about you, an' also because of what he told me about the killin' of the town marshal somewhere down around this settler-town called Grasshopper ... Mister Lord, you an' the marshal was close friends, so tell me: Is it possible he got killed snoopin' around this settler-town because he thought someone down there might be rustling livestock?'

Andy nodded his head. 'The night he was killed we met in the cafe. He told me he was goin' to come down here at night and look around.'

'Did he suspect anyone in particular, Mister Lord?'

'If he did, Marshal, he didn't mention that to me. But he was sure there was some kind of rustling ring operating in his bailiwick.'

The federal peace officer went over to lean

62

with one arm upon the rump of a wheel horse. 'At the Grasshopper settlement?'

Andy shrugged. 'Yes; at least he was interested in those folks. If you'll get inside, Marshal, we can make it down to the way-station and you can talk to the man who runs it. He is about a half mile north and upon the opposite side of the road from the settlement. He's hinted to me there are things goin' on over there that he don't think much of.'

Marshal Lavender smiled, shoved out a hand, then went past to climb into the coach. Andy went up over the wheel to his seat, freed the lines, eased off the binders and talked the horses into moving back to the south roadway.

The night was turning cool. By the time they were within sight of the way-station more than two hours later, it was downright cold.

Ezra had a pair of old carriage lamps lighted on each side of the entrance doorway to his rude log building, and as soon as Andy climbed down to stamp his legs against the cold Ezra's two 'breed sons appeared to briskly work at removing the horses.

Inside, the log building was almost too hot from a large log fire on a stone hearth. Ezra came forward beaming. His woman had been keeping supper warm he said, and looked slightly askance at Andy. 'The last time you was this late, was that time a gully-washer taken out half the road from Deadwood ... Gents, the first drink is on the house.' Ezra beamed a big smile at the federal marshal, his little eyes lost in folds of flesh. He shoved out a ham-sized hand. 'My name is Ezra Kamp—spelt with a *K*.'

Jeff Lavender pumped the hand and did not bat an eye as he replied with a bald lie, 'Proud to make your acquaintance Mister Kamp. My name is John Luther.'

They were at the old rough-log bar having a drink when one of Ezra's sons appeared with the little wooden box in his hand. He looked from Andy to his father as he said, 'Is this what Mister Kinnon was supposed to send down, Paw?'

Andy took the little box, placed it atop the bar and told Kamp he had entirely overlooked bringing the box in with him.

Ezra's little eyes went to the box and remained there until he lifted it to shove it beneath the bar. 'Just some horse bits,' he told his guests, and moved to re-fill their cups as his son left the room without making a sound.

There was a tantalising smell of food beginning to fill the big room with its lanterns on wall-pegs and its pair of large trestle-tables with individual benches around them.

Ezra went out back. Andy heard him speaking in some language Andy guessed had to be Crow, then he returned rubbing his hands

64

together as he took them to one of the tables. 'It'll be along in a couple of minutes, gents. Set. Just set and get comfortable. My woman makes the best spiced antelope steak you ever tasted in your lives.'

CHAPTER SEVEN

SURPRISES FOR ANDY LORD

Ezra ate supper with them and he had not exaggerated, his woman was a fine cook. Not everyone could make antelope tender, nor could everyone season it so there was no gaminess, but she could.

The U.S. Deputy Marshal commented on that and Ezra beamed as though the compliment had been directed toward him. 'Mighty fine woman,' he stated. 'Don't speak English, but she's right decent and thoughtful and kind, and, for an In'ian she's got a good sense of humour. Cost me fourteen good horses and I got to tell you gents, never in my life regretted it. We been together now for close to twenty-five years.'

Andy ate and listened, and was both surprised and pleased at the way Kamp held forth about the virtues of his woman for so long. It was unusual.

The deputy marshal's mournful countenance had a pair of shrewd, sly eyes. He said, 'I expect she does her grub-buying at that settlement I saw when we turned in out front. It's right handy.'

Ezra paused ladling hot beef broth into his mouth, but only very briefly. He shot Andy a quick look, then turned his attention back to the lawman. 'Well, no sir, we don't have no truck with them folks. We do our buyin' up at Deadwood—stock up pretty heavy each time then we don't have to go up there too often.'

The mournful-looking man raised his brows a little. 'But that place would be closer.'

Andy went right on eating. He knew what the lawman was doing and was impressed by the way he went about it.

'Closer,' Ezra Kamp agreed, pushing his empty bowl aside and reaching for the platter of sliced meat. 'That's a settler-town, Mister Luther. We don't have much truck with them, and they pretty much leave us alone. It's not that I'm against settlers so much as it's a fact that the quality of those folks is worse even than it is among most emigrants.'

'Mister Luther' sat back looking at Ezra, showing mild interest in his face. 'You're close to them,' he said. 'I'd guess that if you got no use for them, why then you must have seen things you didn't approve of.'

That, of course, was true, but this time Ezra

was not to be led into volunteering much. 'Enough,' he said cryptically, and changed the subject. 'Andy, there was a trader through a few days ago. I sent him on up to talk to Mister Kinnon. He had some mighty fine big young mules in his tradin' string and the company could sure use a few good stout mules.'

Andy was finished with the meal. He leaned on the table as he nodded. 'You did right, but knowing how tight Charley is I doubt that he'd buy anything right now.'

The federal lawman got into this conversation without difficulty. 'Did that trader come from over yonder at the settlement?'

Ezra looked at the tall, slightly stooped man for a long moment before replying, acting almost as though it was beginning to dawn on him that the passenger had more than a casual interest. 'No, he come straight up the road through the mountains from Wellington. I told him he might could do a little business over yonder and he shook his head. Didn't say why he wouldn't go over there, just shook his head.'

Now, the federal officer asked a question that probably confirmed Kamp's earlier suspicion. He said, 'You're in about as good a position as a man can be in to see folks goin' and comin' over there, Mister Kamp. Have you seen bands of livestock, horses and mules, being driven into the settlement or out of it?'

Ezra put down his eating utensils and stared.

67

His mighty shoulders hunched slightly as he leaned on the table to reply. 'Mister Luther, it's an emigrant settlement. They come and go over yonder. Not all of 'em. There's a feller owns the general store and the blacksmith an' a few others got businesses over at the Grasshopper settlement. It's nothin' more than a stop-over for clodhoppers comin' into the basin from the south, southeast or maybe the southwest so there's always comings and goings.'

'Mister Luther' did not yield an inch. Looking directly back he said, 'You never bought any animals from over there?'

Ezra shook his head. 'No sir, I never did, an' I'll tell you why . . .' Ezra paused to shoot a look in Andy Lord's direction. 'A man can get shot easily as it is, but if somebody rode up to a stranger whose horse has just been stolen and he happens to be riding an animal with the stranger's brand . . . No sir, I have as little to do with those folks as I can. I always offer to help 'em when I can; being doing that for years, but I never been over to their village and don't expect to, either.'

'Mister Luther's' recessed eyes showed an ironic expression. 'They got horsethieves over there, then; is that what you're saying Mister Kamp?'

Andy fidgeted. The federal marshal had already established by insinuation that Kamp thought there were horsethieves across the road.

Why was he insisting on an outright statement of this fact?

Kamp continued to lean oaken arms atop the table as he regarded the tall, lean man. Finally he countered 'Mister Luther's' question with one of his own. 'You're just passin' through, I take it,' he said gruffly, not taking his eyes off the man opposite him at the table. 'Or did I figure that wrong, Mister Luther?'

The lawman's eyes showed new light. He seemed to be enjoying this roundabout conversation. 'Gettin' to know the country, Mister Kamp,' he said, then added something that surprised and interested Andy Lord. 'I been on the far side of the mountains, down around Wellington, and I been east of here to a place called River Crossing, which is a settler-town too. An' the most interesting thing, Mister Kamp, is that west of here close against the mountains I saw as fine a standing network of peeled-log corrals hid back in the timber as you ever saw. An' they are being used right regular. Shod horses and barefoot horses, and mules, been run through them.'

When 'Mister Luther' finished Ezra turned slowly toward Andy. He seemed about to speak, then decided not to and arose as he said, 'I'll fetch the coffee pot.'

After Ezra had left the room Andy turned on the federal lawman. 'I guess you told the truth when you told me up at that turn-out you didn't trust folks ... because you also told me you didn't know this country and hadn't been in it before.'

The mournful-looking lean man smiled at Andy. 'That's right, Mister Lord. I don't trust anybody, and that includes someone the sawbones up in Deadwood swore up and down was trustworthy. But I didn't lie to you; I never was in this part of the country before ... before two weeks back. For those two weeks I scouted up this south country, then I went up to find the marshal—the gent that got killed down here—and now I'm tryin' to satisfy myself I can trust Mister Kamp and you, and right now, the way he run out of the room, I'm ready to write him off.'

The lawman nodded in the direction of the door their host had disappeared through and lowered his voice as he said, 'I told him about the log corrals just to see if he would suddenly decide he needed a drink or something. Mister Lord, if you got doubts all you got to do is go outside, stand in the darkness and wait—if either one of those big, husky 'breeds I saw when we arrived here goes loping across the road in the direction of the settler-town ...' Jeff Lavender made a wise, knowing smile and faced forward to continue eating his meal.

For seconds Andy sat where he was, then, with a growl he got to his feet and left by the massive oaken front door. What Ezra would

70

think when he returned to the table and found Andy not there did not concern Andy very much as he went out where the stagecoach was standing, its tongue on the ground, looking abandoned and forlorn in the moonlight. He leaned on the far side gazing down where a few lights showed at the emigrant settlement.

The lawman's trick had obviously been tried on Ezra Kamp to see whether or not he would send one of his sons to the settlement with a warning that a stranger had been prowling in the territory. Ezra had indeed left the room, but while that had seemed suspicious to the federal lawman, it did not necessarily have to mean much.

Andy stood a long time in the increasing chill of night. There was very little to listen to and except for the lights southward and across the road, there was little to look at until he heard the high, wild sound of a V of geese flying overhead and he watched them pass in front of the moon, an eerie sight. Ground birds roosted at night. Supposedly geese did too, but this was not the first flight he had seen late at night.

As he brought his head down and glanced in the direction of the settlement again, he saw a man moving toward the distant lights. He was on foot, and although poor visibility and distance made a positive identification impossible, Andy's heart sank as he thought he could make out one of Ezra's burly sons. He

71

watched as long as the silhouette was in sight, then shifted position and shoved both hands deep into pockets.

His breath was steaming as he turned and walked heavily back in the direction of the way-station. For some reason it annoyed him that Marshal Lavender had set a little trap and, using Andy to make sure it had worked, had implicated Ezra Kamp in something Andy did not like to think about—large scale horse-stealing.

When he entered the building the table had been cleared. He heard voices from the saloon-section of the way-station and went to the door where the federal lawman and Ezra were seated near a roaring little fire drinking whisky and exchanging stories of their earlier lives.

They looked up as Andy came through the doorway. Ezra promptly got to his feet and went to the bar to fill a glass of half-whisky, half-water, and hand it to Andy while beaming a wide smile in a flushed face.

Before either Andy or Ezra could speak the lawman put words into Andy's mouth. 'Well, how were the horses, Mister Lord?'

He had told Ezra Andy had gone out to look in on the livestock, a perfectly natural thing for a man to do, and as Andy pushed up a smile to match their host's smile, he said, 'Everything seems to be fine.'

72

He then took a chair near the other two men, felt the heat against his cold body, and shoved out both legs, crossed them at the ankles, and instead of drinking the watered whisky, held the glass in one hand while gazing into the fire.

Ezra had been interrupted in the middle of a story when Andy had returned, but now as he sat comfortably watching the flames he picked up where the interruption had distracted him, and concluded the tale with a laugh.

It had been the kind of rollicking tale men exchange when their tongues and inhibitions had been loosened by whisky in a hot room around a fire, after having eaten all they could hold. What made Andy's solemn look grow longer was that, unfortunately, the story had to do with Ezra going on a horse raid with the Crow Indians years back, when he had been courting his woman.

Andy considered the whisky. To a listener like Jeff Lavender, even though he was smiling and relaxed, seemingly in sympathy with their host, a story of stealing horses was about the worst possible experience a man could dredge up and talk about.

Lavender put a sardonic gaze on Andy. He was still wearing the little smile. 'Cold out?' he asked.

Andy nodded. 'Yeah, and getting colder.' He then put his attention upon Ezra as he said, 'Nothing going back up north?'

Ezra sighed and put his cup of watered whisky aside. 'Yeah. Some light freight for the general store. I'll go see if the boys stowed it in the boot. If not I'll tell 'em to.' Ezra arose, still looking at Andy. 'You want the horses put on now?'

Andy nodded. 'Yes. I'm not a schedule but I'd ought to get back anyhow.'

Ezra went stamping through another room to find his hat and coat and muffler, then they heard him leave the building and close a heavy door after himself.

At once Marshal Lavender's gaze went to Andy's face. 'Well . . . did someone leave here heading over there?'

Andy continued to look into the fire as he replied, 'There was a man out there but he was too far off for me to make him out very well.'

'Going toward the settlement?'

Andy grudgingly nodded. 'Yeah.'

The lawman's droopy moustache raised to disclose big, strong white teeth. 'Thanks, Mister Lord.'

Andy ignored that to ask a question. 'Are you goin' to stay here or go back with me?'

'Go back. I got to have a saddle horse for what else I got to do.'

Andy pulled his gaze away from the fire. 'Marshal . . . Lew Brant knew this country backwards and forwards, and he got killed.'

'Yes, I know, and I'll be right careful. Now

74

tell me something, Mister Lord: Would there be any way to anticipate a raid? I don't want to set out there for a long time in the cold and wind and all if I don't have to.'

Andy shrugged. He had seen horses and mules being driven west in broad daylight, and quite possibly Lew Brant had stumbled onto something in the darkness. He said, 'Not that I know about, Marshal. What you really need is someone from over there.'

Lavender's tough smile about that was missed by his companion, who was again staring into the fire. 'About as much chance of me roundin' up someone from the settlement to inform against someone else from over there as there is of me flyin' to the moon.'

Andy would not have argued with that. 'If you finished your drink an' settled up with 'em for supper and all, I think we'd better be heading back.'

Outside with steam rising from their normal breathing, four big, strong company horses had already been put on the tongue. Ezra and his two stalwart sons were going over the hitch for a final inspection. Andy gazed at his sons. They had the same muscled-up build, were about the same height and as far as Andy could determine, from the rear it could have been either one of them who had run from the way-station yard or it could just as easily have been a third person. He was considering ways to ask Ezra if there had been another man at the way-station this evening when one of the younger men diverted him by drawing his attention to the light freight—several wooden boxes nailed closed—which had been tied securely to the rear boot.

Ezra shook Marshal Lavender's hand and beamed a broad smile at him. Ezra's face was flushed and it was not entirely from the heat inside the way-station.

Andy buttoned up, pulled on his gauntlets, looked around as was his custom to be sure he had free-way when he climbed to the high seat to move out, then nodded to the Kamps and went up hand over hand to his position.

As he loosened the lines and reared back to kick off the binders he watched the two younger men turn and head for the building. He saw Ezra standing down there looking up at him, and called down to him. 'Keep you powder dry.'

The massively powerful older man showed his teeth in a laugh. 'You too.'

Andy did not have to cramp the forewheels, he had ample turning ground. He cast a final look back, at the way-station and the more distant emigrant settlement, then straightened around and concentrated on driving. He was in no hurry but even had he been he still would not have jumped his horses out before they were ready for it.

He drove at a slogging walk for two miles then had his hitch pick up the gait a little. The cold was not getting any worse but it did not get any better either, although they were heading into the summery time of year when there would be an occasional warm night as the season advanced.

The moon was gone by the time they rattled and rocked past the lay-by where they had watered the horses on the trip down. This time they did not stop, there was no need to.

CHAPTER EIGHT

A MANIPULATOR

Andy had a run west and one north before he saw the federal lawman again. He was at the cafe having supper when Marshal Lavender walked in looking tired and dusty. They exchanged a nod and Lavender took a seat farther down the counter and ordered.

Andy finished first, went outside where he encountered another company driver and the foreman of the yard. They talked a while about the weather, the condition of the roads, and the number of runs they each had to make, then the other two company men went on up in the direction of the saloon and card room.

77

Andy was about to step down and cross the road on his way to the company bunkhouse when Marshal Lavender emerged from the cafe and said, 'Nice night.' Lavender then used a very sharp knife to cut off a suitable corner of his cut plug and settle it into his cheek. As he snapped the knife closed and also put up the tobacco plug he looked at Andy Lord. After a time he spoke dryly.

'An old cowman from northeast of Deadwood lost some using horses a week or so back.'

Andy nodded, he remembered the incident.

'Well, a neighbour of his was raided last night. I happened to be over on the east range, but I was camped near a little spring and bedded down, so I slept through everything, even though the boys drivin' that latest bunch of stolen horses passed within a half mile of me.'

Andy, wondering where this was going, leaned upon an upright because he already knew that when the U.S. marshal started talking he did not hurry.

'Now then,' said the federal lawman, smiling a little. 'I know where they took those horses, Mister Lord, and although I didn't get a real good look at the men—there were four of 'em—I'll bet you a new hat you know two of them better'n I do. I think you saw one of 'em leave the way-station the other night.'

Andy held up a hand. 'Why don't you just

spit it out, Marshal?' he asked irritably.

Lavender was an obliging individual. 'All right, Mister Lord. I'm betting the two I saw were Mister Kamp's sons.'

Andy pondered that for a moment. 'You can lose a lot of bets like that,' he told the lawman. 'You said you couldn't identify them.'

Lavender spat then smiled slightly in the gloom. 'They are friends of yours.'

'Not really, Mister Lavender, more like acquaintances. But I think you're jumping to a lot of conclusions that could darn well be wrong.'

Lavender turned aside to expectorate again, then he said, 'You're dead right. Tell you what I'd like to do. You and me go back down there a-horseback in the middle of the night and see if they got any horses in that hidden corral. I already made that trip once today. I'd sooner go to bed, but a man's got to do what he thinks is best, eh? Would it be possible for you to meet me down at the liverybarn in, say, an hour?'

Andy looked steadily at the lawman for a long time without making a sound. Eventually, though, he found his tongue. 'You'll have to go alone or find someone else, I've got runs to make.'

Lavender considered that, then nodded and walked briskly away leaving Andy hanging there, braced for an argument which never materialised. One thing was a lead pipe cinch, a man would have to be around the federal marshal a long time to understand him.

But at least this time Marshal Lavender had not manipulated anyone. He had tried to, but it hadn't worked, and it was a fact that Andy had schedules to keep—not tonight and in fact not until late tomorrow morning, but the day after tomorrow he was scheduled to go north on a two-day run.

He was passing Charley Kinnon's lighted office on his way to the bunkhouse out back when Doctor Brady emerged from the office and without seeing Lord, dusted cigar ash from off his vest and started towards his cottage.

Andy was half-way across the yard when Charley appeared in the rear doorway of his office. He made sure it was Andy out there then he called, 'Hey; you got a minute?'

Andy turned back, entered the lighted office, had to squeeze his eyes against the abrupt change, and Charley said, 'I got Buster Munzer to take your run west in the morning and Al Bartlet to take your two-day run up north.'

Andy stopped with his back to the stove staring toward the desk. Charley seated himself and reached for a crockery mug of lukewarm coffee. He met Andy's stare without difficulty. 'Mister McLaughlin's been snooping around today, lookin' at the schedules, timetables, reports, expense sheets and whatnot. He couldn't seem to find anything wrong except that I've been using one of my drivers more than the others—you. He didn't approve of that. By gawd this is the first time that dour old goat said men could be overworked. Anyway, you're off tonight and for the next couple of days.'

Andy scowled. 'Whether I like it or not?'

'Whether you like it or not,' stated Kinnon, then leaned back with his cup. 'McLaughlin's not only chairman of the company, he's also the biggest shareholder. When McLaughlin says jump folks ask how high.'

Andy stood a while longer eyeing Kinnon, then smiled and left the office. He certainly did not object to a couple of days of loafing in the sun. It was unexpected and therefore he had been caught flat-footed, but on his way toward the bunkhouse again, the idea began to please him.

He barely knew Andrew McLaughlin, who was a short, big-boned brawny older man with sandy hair and a mouth like a bear trap. But from what he did know he was inclined to agree with Charley Kinnon's statement that McLaughlin only came down here to find fault, and in this instance the best he could do was pretend to be concerned about one overworked driver.

One of the hostlers came out of the bunkhouse heading out back and before the door closed behind him Andy saw someone sitting on one of the porch chairs, tipped back with booted feet hanging over the railing. He was not particularly concerned, but had he been the light emanating past the briefly opened door would not have lasted long enough for Andy to identify the loafer.

He stepped up onto the worn board porch beneath the bunkhouse overhang and was reaching for the door when a bone-dry voice said, 'I got the horses tied out back in the alley.'

Jeff Lavender unwound up out of the chair in shadowy gloom, stooped, lean figure recognisable as he brushed the back of one hand beneath his hangdog dragoon moustache. 'I got your carbine in the boot on your horse, plus a blanket and poncho.'

Andy's initial reaction of surprise had passed. He stood by the door eyeing the tall man. For a long moment nothing was said between them, not until Andy quietly spoke.

'Marshal, answer a question for me.'

'Be right glad to, Mister Lord.'

'Do you know a man named McLaughlin?'

'Andrew McLaughlin? Yep, I sure do, and by golly you can believe this or not, Mister Lord, here I am in the south part of nowhere and who do I run into at the saloon but Mister McLaughlin. He was—'

'Marshal, how come you to get him to do what he did about me not workin' for the next couple of days?'

'Well, we could be talkin' while we're riding, couldn't we?'

'I'm waiting, Marshal.'

Lavender fished with both hands for his plug, found it and went through his ritual of getting a cud into his face before he answered.

'We go back a long ways, Mister Lord. When he first come west he bought into a Montana cow outfit, then he went back east—and from the rangeboss down his hired men began robbin' him blind. I found most of the cattle and horses, notified him, and helped bring in his riders.'

'So he owed you.'

Lavender nodded with a faint smile. 'Couple of other little things ... Mister Lord, we're wasting good time standin' here.'

Andy gazed dispassionately at Jeff Lavender. An hour back he'd been complimenting himself on avoiding being manipulated by the federal officer. He shook his head; his grandfather had told him one time to always figure the other feller was just as smart as he was, and maybe smarter, and for that reason never to be complacent about out-smarting someone.

'What makes you think I'm going to ride my tailbone raw and maybe get shot at just because you want someone to do some scouting with you tonight?'

Lavender had the answer to that also. 'Lewis Brant,' he said quietly.

Andy remained in position another couple of moments undecided whether to swear or laugh. He did neither. 'I got to get my coat.'

'It's tied atop the blanket on your saddle,' stated the federal officer, who then leaned to spray amber and walked down off the porch in the direction of a small postern gate built into the palisaded rear wall of the corralyard. Andy followed him.

He expected livery horses. Instead, the two strong, muscled-up animals patiently standing out back rigged for riding belonged to the stage company. Andy untied the horse meant for him to ride while shaking his head. McLaughlin again, no doubt.

He shrugged into his blanketcoat when they were a couple of miles south of Deadwood and cast a sidelong glance at his lanky, stooped companion. Marshal Lavender was slouching along with his eyes fixed dead ahead. He had the appearance of a man who was deep in thought so Andy remained silent.

So much for two days of loafing, catching up on his sleep, sewing some buttons on his shirts and greasing his boots with heated oil among other inconsequential things that he'd been putting off for months.

Lavender jettisoned his cud and straightened around as he said, 'Too bad there's no town lawman.'

Andy shrugged about that. A town marshal

84

would not have had the muscle of a deputy U.S. marshal, whose authority entitled him to cross state and territorial borders, to override the decisions of local law officers, and to take prisoners over county lines without extradition papers.

Lavender spoke on a different subject. 'Those folks down yonder got a constable. Did you know that?'

'No. Like I already told you, I have rarely entered their community.'

Lavender was understanding. 'Normally I'd say no one who's followed range ridin' at some time in their life would enter an emigrant settlement unless his horse went lame or something just as bad ... Still, if we knew someone down there...'

'But you're not heading for the settlement,' stated Andy and got a nod of the lawman's head to support the statement.

'No. I expect we might eventually end up over there, but no, we're goin' over to that hidden log corral they got. That's where the stolen horses are.' As he finished speaking Jeff Lavender turned his head. 'In case somethin' should come up tonight that'll require one or the other of us to call to the other feller, my first name is Jeff, an' do you mind if I call you Andy?'

'Don't mind at all,' stated Lord. 'What's likely to come up—Jeff? You got some idea of

85

retrieving those stolen horses?'

Lavender rode along in silence for a while before replying, 'Y'never know, do you? We're not fixing to do business with ribbon and bolt goods pedlars are we? I'd sure like to stampede those horses back north in the direction they came from, but I been at my trade quite a while, Andy, so there's one thing I know to be a plumb fact. A man hadn't ought to ever make more than just a simple plan because if he tries to cover every aspect of what can happen, he's goin' to end up being confused enough not to do anything ... We're just goin' to try and find those horses and, in the process, not be found ourselves.'

Andy thought of his friend. He would like to settle the score for him. He decided to seek an opportunity to do just that.

He also decided that if he had needed a teacher for what he had embarked upon the moment he left town with the federal officer, he probably would have been unable to find a more experienced one.

This was just a feeling he had, but Andy was crowding his forties and had been with people all of those years. He had developed an ability to make sound assessments about his fellow human beings.

Marshal Lavender was a shrewd, sly, self-effacing individual, the kind who had a knack for allowing folks to underestimate him at their peril.

It eventually became possible to skyline the rising hills against a paler, dark sky. Andy knew about where he was, he had hunted down through here years earlier when there had been no emigrant settlement some miles westward. Marshal Lavender did not hesitate. He knew exactly where he was heading despite limited visibility, areas of pure darkness, and the appearance of a countryside that looked different after nightfall than it looked during daylight.

Andy grudgingly admired some of the federal officer's characteristics and traits. He did not particularly admire Lavender's methods of manipulation. Andy had needed no reminder back in Deadwood at the corralyard bunkhouse that Lew Brant should be avenged. It stuck in his craw that in this instance Lavender had used his dead friend's name to get him to ride south.

Lavender suddenly said, 'Yonder. See that spit of trees coming down like an arrowhead? Back up through there no more'n thirty, forty yards.' Lavender leaned on his saddlehorn peering ahead and chewing a fresh cud. He eventually slouched back against the cantle and smiled over at the man riding with him.

'For your sake and their paw's sake I hope those sons of Ezra Kamp aren't up ahead.'

Andy agreed in strong silence. He had thought he had caught the very brief but

87

brilliant flash of a fire part way up the yonder slope in among the trees. He had waited patiently for the light to show again, but it never did.

One thing he felt confident of, was that if the stolen horses were up ahead in a hidden set of corrals there would be men somewhere close by, and because it was cold now, and perhaps because they felt it would be safe to do so, they would light a warming fire.

CHAPTER NINE

HORSES AND MEN

Andy mentioned what he thought he had seen up the slope above the area where Jeff had said the corrals were situated, and the federal peace officer veered farther west, maintaining their route across a tangled matting of stirrup-high green grass which muffled the sound of their passing.

They were too far out to be seen, unless of course the horsethieves had a man out a ways watching the back trail. They may have had one, but by the time Andy and his companion reached the timber they had been riding on a long-spending angle which kept them well away from the vicinity of the corrals.

As they were dismounting to lead their animals among the trees to be hidden Andy said, 'If someone ran off that old gaffer's horses last night—why in hell hasn't he rounded up a posse and come down their trail?'

Jeff Lavender was moving deeper among the huge trees as he answered. 'Because I told him not to. There's no sense to the notion that a herd of hard-riding men from up around Deadwood can come storming down to that emigrant settlement, take whatever they want includin' those horses up yonder—and not lose half their party ... Your friend knew his way around, and he didn't make it.' Lavender paused and faced Andy. 'Even the folks down here who aren't involved with a rustling ring, know by now just about how welcome they are in livestock country. Maybe they wouldn't have a watcher out, but sure as hell if the settlement was attacked they'd fight. Andy, I don't want a war, I just want whoever's the head of this rustling operation—and maybe a few others. From here on we'd better not even whisper.'

Lavender was a seasoned stalker even in the dark. He was also a cautious one. Andy did not smell anything but his companion stopped facing southward toward open country and wrinkled his nose. 'Tobacco smoke,' he whispered, and instead of pressing on past this area he turned toward the source of that aroma.

Andy saw the man's hunched shoulders

89

inside an old moth-eaten bearskin coat that went below his knees. The man was sitting on a big punky old deadfall smoking a little pipe and indifferently watching the faintly starlighted open country northward.

Lavender held a hand back to stop Andy. He then continued ahead by himself. Andy sank to one knee leaning on his Winchester. Once, the scruffy figure in the old skin coat turned, but not because he had heard or sensed the lawman stalking him, to knock dottle from his pipe, pocket the little thing and get to his feet to mightily stretch, scratch, re-set a shapeless old cavalry campaign hat complete with acorn hatband, and to lustily clear his pipe and expectorate with considerable force before looking around, studying the darkness where Andy was barely breathing, then face ahead and resume his sitting posture on the rotting old log.

He was a burly, large, darkly bearded man whose hairline was no more than three inches above his eyebrows. By weak starlight Andy's impression of the watcher was that he would have looked more at home in the opening to a cave eating raw meat and wearing a hair-out skin of some kind instead of clothing.

During the sentry's restless movements Andy had lost track of the federal officer. Now, he tried to find him. Movement was all he watched for since in among the big trees shadows were

90

likely to resemble anything including two-legged creatures, as long as they did not move.

But there was no movement.

From a considerable distance Andy heard a horse whinny. Otherwise the silence was deep and unending. He settled a little lower trying to locate Marshal Lavender by backgrounding him. He did no better here either, so he straightened back up, remained on one knee clutching the saddlegun, and waited.

It seemed to be a very long wait before a little muffled sound yanked Andy's attention to the rounded slouching figure in the old skin coat sitting on the log.

For a moment the seated man remained in place. Then he began to list to his left as though overcome with sleep, except that he continued to fall until Andy could no longer see him because he had collapsed down in front of the big log he had been sitting upon.

There still was no sign of Marshal Lavender. Andy glanced over his shoulder, restless and a little anxious. He did not move except to turn his head from time to time. It seemed that hours had passed before the tall, lean lawman came over beside Andy and sat down cross-legged without making a sound. He held up an old sixgun which no longer had any of its original bluing left, an 'Arkansas toothpick' with a hollow-ground blade as sharp as a razor, and finally showed Andy a massive, beautifully engraved gold pocket watch on a gold chain. He pocketed the watch and tossed the knife and sixgun backwards into the darkness.

Andy was staring. 'Did you kill him?'

Lavender put a sardonic look upon his companion. 'No, but it's not a bad idea. I hit him in the back of the head with a rock from a distance of about three feet.'

Andy looked down toward the deadfall. 'How long will he be out?'

'Maybe not as long as you'd like, but I tied him like a turkey and gagged him with his bandana and his handkerchief.'

'We been here a long time, Marshal.'

Lavender was getting to his feet and brushing off pine needles when he said, 'It just seemed like a long time. Anyway, I got an iron rule—don't ever leave one of them behind you ... Let's go.'

Now, the lawman began angling up the slope on their left. He observed caution as Andy also did but they could have fallen flat and the sound would not have carried ten feet because of the carpet of fresh needles on top and decomposing needles beneath the uppermost layers which had been accumulating in this place for generations. A ground cover of cotton could not have absorbed sound as well.

Andy smelled wood smoke. His companion halted, faded from sight around a big tree and when Andy appeared he touched him and pointed. Andy also stepped behind a big tree.

The fire was small and burning brightly. If the three men sitting around it hunched against the cold while drinking coffee from tin cups had been able to make their fire of only dry faggots it would have snapped and crackled less. Also, it would have smoked less.

Lavender watched for a long time. So long that Andy peered apprehensively around. Three men up ahead through the trees at their small warming-fire, and one back yonder knocked senseless by a rock was the number of men the marshal had told him were responsible for this latest horse-raid, but Lewis Brant had been killed somewhere around here, and he too had been a wily, seasoned manhunter. Maybe the four men who had stolen the horses and who had brought them down here were only part of a larger outlaw band. Equally as possible was the prospect of other men appearing soon to take over from the men up ahead.

Marshal Lavender glided over to join Andy. 'From in back do any of them look familiar to you?'

Andy scowled at the innuendo, then leaned to make a more prolonged and careful study. But those men were also bundled inside coats. He shook his head at the federal officer.

Lavender did not seem to have expected anything different. 'Just didn't want you to get tongue-tied when the trouble starts,' he said.

Andy eyed the older man. 'You want to rush them?'

Lavender shook his head. 'No. You stay where you are like you did back yonder. But there's always the chance of a mistake. If any of them try to break away heading your way, shoot them. All right?'

'Marshal, we don't know for a fact there are stolen horses up ahead somewhere, and we don't know these are the four men who ran them down here.'

Lavender was not troubled. 'Four men stole the horses. There are four men here keeping watch over them. What more proof do you want? And one other thing; it'll be dawn in another hour or two. If we don't get those men before dawn sure as I'm standin' here whispering to you, they are goin' to line those horses out and head west with them—and we'll be left holding the sack.'

Andy watched the tall man glide away from him with mild wonder. He had seemed so shrewd and clever other times; how could he say that because four raiders had stolen the horses and there were four men here now, they had to be the same four?

Up ahead a man coughed long and hard, breaking across Andy's thoughts. He eased around, saw a way to advance and moved undetected to within a few hundred feet of the

94

fire. Now, one man was lying flat out on the ground with a blanket over him.

There was no sign of Lavender but that bothered Andy less now than it had earlier. In fact quite abruptly he forgot Lavender altogether. A barrel-shaped bearded man wearing one of the most disreputable hats Andy had ever seen, stood up from the fire letting an old army blanket drop from his shoulders as he said, 'All right. Time to take over from Will.'

Another man muttered something Andy could not understand. The standing man replied in the same carelessly loud voice. 'I know that. I been sayin' it all day. But in case I'm wrong and they did try to track us down here, sure as hell they wouldn't ride up in plain daylight, so we got to keep watch for 'em in the night ... Anyway, it'll be light directly and we can be on our way.'

Without warning a light stick fell across Andy's shoulder and he whirled pulling up the carbine to aim it. Marshal Lavender ignored the impression he'd made and made a gesture of throat-cutting, pointed at the thick man who was leaving the fire now, then made another gesture—toward the fire this time, and patted his holstered Colt, nodded at Andy, and faded from sight again.

Lavender's meaning had seemed to indicate that he wanted Andy to capture the two men still hunkering by the fire. His earlier throat-cutting gesture could have been taken literally or not. If not, then it had simply implied that he would take care of the man who was now walking away to relieve the sentry Lavender had knocked senseless and left tied. Andy did not dwell very long upon the opposite implication—an actual throat-cutting.

He watched the relief-horsethief pass south of his big trees and tried to hear his more distant footfalls afterwards, but failed and had to give his shoulder a figurative shrug; with that man behind him somewhere, Andy had to believe Jeff Lavender could handle him. Andy's attention was now upon the remaining two outlaws sitting like mummies by the fire, each of them with a blanket around his shoulders.

A horse whinnied to the right and up ahead somewhere. Andy had been in the process of approaching the nearest outlaw from behind, but when that noise broke the stillness both men by the fire came abruptly alive, raised their heads and peered back toward the source of the sound.

Andy faded out behind a tree and sank to one knee not willing to risk a peek but straining to hear as one of the outlaws prodigiously yawned then said, 'Nobody's comin' for Chris'sake. Even if they did they couldn't find this place in the darkness. I still figure we should have kept right on and got rid of those darned horses even if we'd had to go yonder in broad daylight. Who the hell that far away would know anything?'

Instead of replying to the question, the second horsethief was rolling a cigarette when he offered his own independent view. 'It's too far, takin' 'em over to that town where they take 'em off our hands. I been sayin' all along we could push 'em straight south, down through the mountains and out onto the south desert and get shed of 'em for as much money and at half the bother and time.'

The first man blew out a noisy big breath as he spoke again. 'Can't keep this up much longer around here anyway, Bud. I'll tell you flat out right up to the day Flander snuck up on that town marshal and blasted him I was worried that someone up in Deadwood would round up a big posse and come down our back trail. Even with the town marshal dead, an' even with folks up in the Deadwood country as leaderless as Ezra says they are, we've used up all our time around here. We got to move along, somewhere else a hell of a distance from here.'

The second man was about to speak when a muffled jolt, more like a reverberation than an actual sound, caused Andy as well as the outlaws out through the trees in their tiny glade to swing eastward and half come up to their feet.

Andy tried to guess what had made that sound. It was rather as though a large horse had fallen to the ground, a sound like that, with no sharpness and no echo.

Both the outlaws were crouching, blankets off and hands upon gunhandles. The one who had been called Bud softly said, 'Sounded like a tree fallin' or something like that.' As though reassured by his own voice he straightened up slightly and let his right hand hang at his side. 'It wasn't nothin' to worry about or Flander would have fired off a round or yelled.'

Andy did not hear the other man's reply. He had been looking at the man who had murdered Lew Brant. It had been the man named Flander, the gorilla-like outlaw with the disreputable old hat who had gone back to relieve the man Lavender had knocked senseless.

Andy twisted from the waist to look back through the gloom and timber but there was no sign of Flander. He briefly debated with himself whether to drop back and see if he could come in behind Flander, thus helping Jeff Lavender because he was certain Lavender meant to waylay this outlaw too, or whether to do as Lavender had wanted and try to capture the pair of men up ahead of him.

With reluctance he faced forward. The man known as Bud was leaning, poking twigs into the little fire. His back was to Andy. The other man, opposite Bud, was facing in Andy's direction. When the fire blazed up the man facing Andy raised a hand to his face and squeezed his eyes nearly closed. He had been temporarily blinded.

Andy stepped from behind his tree directly into the view of the blinded man, whom he ignored as he walked stealthily toward Bud whose back was still to him and who was still sifting through several armloads of odd length bits of firewood.

Andy swept his right hand downward, then upwards holding his sixgun. When the barrel descended Bud was beginning to straighten up. He arose directly beneath the steel barrel and collapsed as though his body had no bones in it.

CHAPTER TEN

IN THE TIMBER

The outlaw who had been temporarily blinded when the fire had flared, either heard Bud grunt as he fell, or his blindness had been dissipating as Andy approached from the trees. In either case he bellowed, went for his sixgun and hurled himself sideways as he fired.

The bullet struck a tree trunk with a meaty sound. Andy was flat down when he returned the fire but as before the outlaw had sprinted sideways, to his right. He and Andy fired simultaneously and again neither was injured.

Now, the embattled horsethief turned and launched himself through the air past the first row of trees across the small clearing.

Andy wanted to swear. He could no longer see his adversary and had no intention of springing up and charging across the clearing to get over there. Without warning a gun blasted from the trees behind Andy Lord. His surprise was complete because he saw soil explode six inches to his left, and his first thought, which was that Jeff Lavender had returned at the sound of firing, was wrong. Lavender would not fire that close to Andy Lord. It had to be the big, bearlike man with the beard, the one named Flander who had gone out to relieve the sentry Jeff had tied like a shoat.

Andy knocked the coffee pot into the fire, and as flames diminished and steam hissed, he sprang up into a crouch and started running.

Flander bawled something, probably a taunt, and fired again. This time the slug spewed needles, tiny pebbles and dirt over Andy's lower legs. It was almost as though Flander wanted to prolong this game.

Andy didn't; he swung to watch for muzzleblast and when it came with Flander's third shot, Andy drilled a bullet to the left of the muzzle-flame, to the right, and the last one went straight down the middle. All three shots had been so closely spaced they sounded more like bullets from a Gatling gun than from a single-shot Colt revolver.

Andy got in among the trees, there was no more gunfire, but as the silence settled where receding echoes had been, Andy was sure he heard riders approaching, coming up fast from the direction of the settlement. He worried about Marshal Lavender. He also worried about Andrew Lord; those riders were coming west out beyond the trees and they would probably break up through the timber about where Andy was standing.

They had not been attracted by gunfire; they probably had been approaching from the direction of the emigrant settlement when all hell broke loose, and they had spurred their animals.

Part of the careless conversation of the outlaws had to do with men coming to take over the horse-drive. Andy was facing the sound of the newcomers as he decided who they had to be.

He did not see them even though he heard them slackening their gait before turning up into the timber. Behind him at the steaming fire the man named Bud was stirring. Andy spared one moment to look back out there through the trees. Bud would not be of much help to the newcomers, he was so groggy he could not get off the ground.

Andy leathered the sixgun, raised the carbine belt-buckle high, cocked it, and stood holding it

101

in both hands as he awaited the first sighting of someone charging past on horseback.

From the eastward darkness a man bellowed. Survival instinct warned Andy not to allow this to divert him. There was something large and thick sashaying toward him among the trees. The rider was concentrating on not allowing his twisting, turning mount to brush him off by going saddle-horn high beneath a tree limb. He did not see Andy, who was motionless as he waited, and who blended perfectly with his rugged surroundings.

The same roar of a bellow sounded, but this time it was a little closer, on Andy's right. He dared not even look aside, one of those oncoming riders was reining wildly to his left. He was holding a cocked Colt high in his right fist when Andy snugged his finger inside the Winchester's trigger-guard. The rider was suddenly reining in the opposite direction to avoid another big tree when Andy fired.

The fireball and thunder of a gunshot practically in the excited horse's face made him fling up his head, jam his forelegs stiffly, and squat in back. The effect of this was to catapult the rider over the horse's head on the right side. The man let go with a high, wavery outcry. He soared in front of Andy Lord like an oversized, ungainly bird. His sixgun came down before the man did. The horse had whirled to flee but had stepped on his own reins which jerked him to a

102

painful halt. He stood shaking with fear, believing himself to be restricted.

Andy ignored the horse. There were other riders crashing through the underbrush and around the trees on both sides of him, but they were farther away. He wondered for a fleeting moment where Jeff Lavender was, then he stepped up beside the writhing man on the ground whose mouth and eyes were wide open as he struggled to catch a breath of the wind that had been knocked out of him.

He knew him ... Lavender had been right and perhaps in his heart Andy had known this because as he gazed at the husky younger man at his feet he swore and shook his head. The breathless man was one of Ezra Kamp's 'breed sons. Andy did not know which one and did not remember their names, but he had seen both of them many times and without a doubt he was looking at one of them now.

He knelt, hoisted the youth, braced him with one knee and beat him hard on the back several times. As the younger man's breath returned he gulped and rolled his eyes. Andy arose and stepped a yard away as he said, 'Lie flat on your belly and don't move nor make a sound.'

He tied the burly youth using the man's own shellbelt, britches belt and red bandana. As he arose from this someone began shouting a name. 'Ben! Ben! ... *the corrals!*'

Andy considered his position. The riders who

had come up through the trees had turned eastward, perhaps in response to those earlier loud shouts. As far as Andy knew he was closer to the corrals than anyone else. As he turned to trot among the trees westward in the direction he had earlier heard horses, he hoped he was the nearest man. If he wasn't and someone was already down there, he could get himself killed unless he was very careful.

And where the hell was that confounded federal lawman!

He saw the corrals because the log stringers had been meticulously draw-knifed until there was no bark on them, and their pale inner skin shone clearly beyond the darker timber Andy was hastening through. There was a large band of horses in the corrals and they were agitated. Dust rose, horses wheeled and ran, slammed up to reverse themselves and run in a different direction. They bounced off one another hardly noticing. They were frantic with terror from the gunshots.

Andy stopped beside a big Douglas fir to catch his breath and to also look for someone else who might be over here. He saw no one, detected no movement, decided he could not spend the time to make certain he was alone and ducked back and forth toward the front of the corral, which faced north, where the wide pole gate was. Once he was in front of the gate the corrals protected him to some extent from discovery. He utilised every bit of this advantage as he leaned aside the Winchester and fumbled with the log chain and harness snap which held the gate closed.

As he was muscling the big gate open a furious exchange of gunfire erupted far to the east. Andy hoped the outlaws were mistaking one another for enemies in the darkness and confusion of the forest but he would not have wagered a plugged *centavo* that was what all the firing was about. It sounded as though the outlaws had cornered Marshal Lavender.

Andy gave the gate a final, powerful shove to get it wide open, then he did not even look back to see if the horses saw the opening; he went back the way he had come.

The gunfire ended as abruptly as it had erupted. Andy stepped out of the darkness beside the man he had tied. Evidently most of the pain and all of the shock had passed because the dark youth rolled over and sat up looking at his captor. He spoke behind the gag. Andy ignored him and moved ahead to reach a big protective tree. From there he probed the gloom for movement.

By his calculation there were no less than four and perhaps as many as five or six men out through the trees somewhere to the east.

He did not like the odds but he liked the silence even less. When gunfights ended as abruptly as this one had east of the camp and corrals, it was usually because someone's enemy had been taken out.

He heard the stampeding horses. Like most horses they'd had to reconnoitre that wide-open gate before risking a charge past it.

There had been many horses in there. It sounded like there had been even more as the animals headed due north in a wild charge, making the night reverberate as they ran out into open country where they could move even faster.

A man shouted something down about where Lavender had cold-cocked that man in the bearhide coat. There was an answer, then a second answer. Andy edged down closer to starlight and grassland. He was sure whoever the ramrod was had just sent a pair of riders to head off the loose stock and turn it back.

He was right. A pair of hard-riding men broke clear of the timber in flinging pursuit of the escaping animals. Andy waited a moment, watching them, before starting in the direction of the man who had been shouting orders.

He was certain Marshal Lavender was over there somewhere, possibly injured. He had no idea who the ramrod was and at the moment was not very concerned; he just wanted to find the man, if he could. After that events would dictate what came next.

He never made it.

The trees east of the corrals and fire-ring

were not as close together as they were westerly. Also, there seemed to be more blow-downs over here, as though this area caught the first storms of the season. Andy was picking his way with care, stepping over what he could and going around one end or the other of the downed timber too large to be stepped over, and his progress was slow. He had to watch where he put his feet. He also had to try and watch for movement up ahead, but when trouble arrived it did not come from up there, it came from behind Andy Lord.

He was freeing one foot from jammed small logs and had to bend over to work the foot loose at the precise moment someone fired at him from in back and northward, down near where the trees ended and the grassland began.

He wrenched the foot loose and dove face-first into a thorny thicket where additional blow-downs made his landing unpleasant.

Now, he inched to his right and waited. He could not see anything that resembled a human shadow or silhouette and there was no movement, at least none he could see but his view was restricted on both sides by big trees and semi-darkness.

He continued to wait. It dawned on him eventually that the probable reason he could not locate the man who had tried to kill him was because the man was no longer down where he had been . . . He was going far out around Andy

Lord's place of concealment, and eventually would appear directly behind Andy's bush. He squirmed until he could see behind his bush. There was nothing there. Either his adversary had not yet arrived, or he had decided not to pursue this private battle, and perhaps had stealthily crept around to join his friends on Andy's right out through the trees.

Uncertainty heightened fear every time. Andy was sweating like a stud-horse and it was the shank of the night in a country where cold was never any farther than arm's length away. He wanted this assassin. He wanted him alive. He did not believe it would be the man named Flander who had killed Lew Brant but he hoped very hard that it could be.

He belly-crawled from one bush to another bush, angling up the slope in the direction of the forest. He had protection part of the way. He also had to veer hard to his left, which was eastward, or in the direction of those intermittent and furious gunshot exchanges some time earlier. He expected there would be outlaws over there. He had seen two ride away after the loose stock, and he had left one of Ezra Kamp's sons gagged and tied, but there were still at least three men, and perhaps four, over where he was crawling.

In fact if the man Lavender had knocked senseless with a rock had been revived, there could be as many as five men he had to avoid.

He sank flat behind a rounded sandstone mound, heaved a stone as far as he could in the opposite direction, and waited.

Nothing happened. He squirmed completely around to look eastward and until he saw something dully grey two dozen yards back and southward he did not realise that dawn had arrived.

The dull grey object was a carbine barrel. It was all that showed where someone was hunkering down behind a tree. Andy was tempted, but did not fire at the gun barrel. He inched up over the top of his bread-dough shaped sandstone shield, saw a man aiming, and dropped flat as the bullet skived directly across the top of the stone. It fractured from top to bottom. Sandstone had no stopping power.

Andy heard his heart pounding over the slamming echoes of the gunshot. He was pinned down. The gunman in front knew where he was, he could not crawl backwards because that other one was southward where he could see everything from his sheltering tree, and no one yelled at him to throw his weapons away; this was not a fight for supremacy it was a fight to the death.

Where was that damned deputy U.S. marshal!

There was a sound of galloping horses but it was from the east not the north, so he did not believe the mounted outlaws had overtaken the loose stock and were now driving it back toward the corrals.

Someone fired off a shot behind Andy, out through the trees eastward and followed this with an outcry that rang with alarm. He was flat and motionless until he thought he heard his personal adversary running away through the trees and raised his head. It was not the man who had been trying to snipe him, it was another man closer and southward.

Andy looked for his personal assailant. The man chose this same moment to step around a tree looking for Andy.

Lord did not aim, he pointed and squeezed off a shot, levered up very rapidly and tugged off another shot. Both slugs hit the tree on the man's right side. He corrected and fired the third shot at the same moment his enemy fired at him. It was so close the gun-thunder seemed to be one very loud explosion.

The outlaw seemed about to withdraw, to move back behind his tree, but his gestures were sluggish. He touched the tree, braced himself against it with one hand and hung there until the gun fell from his fingers, then he crumpled to the ground.

CHAPTER ELEVEN

A WOMAN AND A WAGON

There was pandemonium to the west somewhere, down in the area of the corrals. Andy waited a long time before moving, even though it appeared that whatever was happening west of him was now the focal point of excitement. Where he was lying he had one dead man in sight, the man who had attempted to back-shoot him from beside a tree. Otherwise there was no sign of anyone else.

He continued to wait, listening to the gunfire and shouting to the west, trying to understand it. His first conclusion was that whoever those riders were who had come racing from the east must have been enemies of the horsethieves, but that was what he preferred to believe. One thing supported his idea, though; whoever those men were they were engaging in a lot of shouting and gunfire down there.

He eased up very slightly and when nothing happened he pushed upwards still more. Still nothing happened so he arose, gripping the Winchester, and began moving toward the man he had shot.

The man had not died instantly. In fact if he could have been helped he might not have died at all. Andy's bullet had shattered an artery. The man had bled to death while all that other uproar was in progress.

He tipped him over with a boot-toe and recognised the bearded, thick-featured face. This was the man his friends had called Flander, the man who had killed Lew Brant if what his friends had said at the fire was true, and they'd had no reason to prevaricate.

He stood a moment longer than he intended to trying to find some measure of satisfaction for the killing, then he turned away, picked his route carefully until he was in sight of the old punky log he and the federal lawman had seen their first adversary sitting on. That man was gone but a short distance onward there was a second dead man. He went over and looked down into a grey face made visible by the broadening dawnlight. This time it was the man who had escaped from the little fire-ring when the fight had started back there.

He had covered considerable distance to reach this place from the fire-site. A scratchy voice spoke suddenly and quietly from ahead through the trees. 'If that feller's shirt is clean fetch it over here, I need some bandaging.'

The shirt was hopelessly filthy. Andy walked ahead until he saw Jeff Lavender propped against a tree, hatless and with blood on his lower body and his trousers. They did not speak as Andy leaned aside the carbine and knelt to look at the wound. Except for the loss of blood the injury was unlikely to result in death, but the bleeding had to be stopped. Andy cut the sleeve from Lavender's shirt and did the same with one of the sleeves from his own shirt, knotted them and made a round-the-body bandage which he could tighten, then he left Lavender and went to Flander for two more sleeves and a clean blue bandana which he took back to reinforce his bandage with and to also place folded over the gash in Lavender's side.

The bleeding diminished. Marshal Lavender was grey and slack. He gestured with one hand. 'I got two, they're back yonder.'

Andy nodded without going to investigate. He hunkered in the dawn chill studying the federal lawman. He did not look capable of moving, let alone sitting a horse. Lavender roused himself and said, 'Who was that went charging past out in the open?'

Andy had no idea but began to push back upright as he answered. 'I don't know, but whoever it was seemed to have caught those horsethieves down by the corrals. There was a lot of gunfire down there.'

Marshal Lavender's head was forward, his chin on his chest. Maybe he had heard Andy but most likely he hadn't. Andy leaned to examine the improvised bandage then took the carbine and started walking back in the

113

direction of the corrals. The furious fight which had been going on down there must have ended while he was working on Marshal Lavender because he heard nothing now.

He came to the place they had left their saddle animals. They were not there which was not much of a surprise. He angled down closer to open country without leaving the shelter and protection of the trees, and not far ahead two men were conversing in normal tones.

Andy reverted to his earlier tactic by pressing in behind trees and moving stealthily until he could see them. One was a thick, tall man. The other one was older, not quite as tall but just as thick. He had a beard which he was perhaps unconsciously tugging on as he spoke.

'Garth'll get it out of them. Anyway, whoever they was sure as hell if they ain't dead back among them trees, they've lit out.'

The tall man said, 'Lit out on what? Only horses I saw when they gave up was headin' home, stirrups flying.'

The shorter man spat, wagged his head and spoke on a different subject. 'You want to know what I think? I think them bastards have been stealin' livestock in all directions and fetchin' 'em here before disposing of them. It wasn't just us they hit.'

The taller man inclined his head. 'Sure sounded that way from what the feller you shot said. I'd like to be down at that settlement

114

about now when Garth rides in with their men walkin' out front with their arms up.'

'Well hell,' responded the shorter man sounding annoyed. 'There's no point in this—if there are any left out here they'll be dead. Let's go down there.'

Andy moved from behind his tree. 'They're not all dead,' he said quietly, and the two strangers whirled to face him. The tall one said, 'Who are you—one of them horse-stealin' sons of—?'

'My name is Andrew Lord. I drive stage out of Deadwood. I came down here with a deputy U.S. marshal lookin' for some horses that were stolen off a ranch north of Deadwood. The marshal got shot; he's leanin' against a tree back yonder. He needs help bad.'

The tall man seemed to accept all this but his companion didn't. 'Federal marshal,' he said scornfully. 'You figure we're stupid enough to let you lead us back among them trees where your friends can shoot us?'

Andy regarded the man stonily. 'There is no one back yonder but a wounded lawman and a couple of corpses. That's the gospel truth.' He pointed. 'You walk behind me with that gun cocked, mister ... The deputy marshal needs help.' Andy eyed them for a moment then turned slowly and started back.

The tall man shouldered past his friend and followed Andy. The other man followed too,

115

but warily eyeing shadows every step of the way. He had a cocked sixgun hanging in his fisted right hand.

When they reached Jeff Lavender both strangers became solicitous, more so when one of them found the badge in Lavender's pocket. The tall man volunteered to go back where they'd left their animals tethered and ride to the settlement for help.

His friend called after him, 'A wagon, Steve,' then he met Andy's gaze and reddened. 'Well, how would you have reacted if someone lookin' like a scarecrow walked up to you right after you'd gone through a battle in the damned trees?'

Andy did not answer, he knelt beside Lavender to see if the bleeding had started again. It hadn't. He gestured for the other man to help him get Lavender stretched out flat on the ground. As they accomplished this the bearded man said, 'I didn't catch your name back yonder.'

'Andy Lord.'

'Yeah. Mine is Toby Gregor. It was MacGregor but my paw dropped the Mac. You drive stage out of Deadwood?'

'Yes.'

Toby Gregor jabbed in Lavender's direction with a thick thumb. 'Just him and you against those horsethieves?' Gregor went to lean on a nearby tree before completing his statement.

116

'Didn't you know how many there was?'

'Yeah, four.'

'Four hell. Maybe there was four when you boys jumped 'em but I counted six includin' one feller who'd been shot off a horse, and a couple of others who went up through the trees like ghosts.'

Andy worried about Lavender lying on cold ground and went looking for something to cover him with. He found a saddleblanket and brought it back. Toby Gregor watched, then said, 'Did you hear us comin' from the east?'

Andy nodded. 'First off I thought it was some horses I turned out of the corral a while back, but they went north.' He lifted his face toward the bearded man. 'Who are you fellers?'

'We're from down around a town called Duryea, you know where it is?'

Andy nodded. He'd driven coach down there a few times in years past but not lately. Duryea was a log-town in a valley about forty miles southeast. They raised a lot of cattle in Duryea Valley. 'I've been there a few times.'

'Yeah. So have those sons of bitches we had the scrap with. We been losing horses down there pretty heavy for the last six months. It got to the place where somethin' had to be done so our Constable Henry Garth took some fellers and after the last raid they started tracking. The tracks led along the base of them mountains south of here. Someone had tried to brush them

117

out but Henry Garth can read the ground like it was a book. He came back to make up a posse and we figured if we came up here in the night we'd stand a better chance of not gettin' killed. But we heard gunfire while we was still a considerable distance off and came on the run.'

Marshal Lavender spoke from beneath the saddleblanket, his voice like a rasp over steel. Until he spoke Andy had thought he was still asleep or unconscious.

'Glad you came along,' he said. 'It got pretty hot there for a while.'

Toby Gregor went over to kneel beside Lavender. 'You caught a pretty good one, Marshal.'

Lavender's grey lips pulled downward in a rueful smile. 'So it seems. I heard part of what you told Andy ... something about a place called Duryea. That's where you gents are from?' Lavender paused. 'You know a man down there named Henry Garth?'

Gregor's eyes widened slightly. 'Sure. He's here with us. He's the Duryea town constable. You know him?'

'Well, I knew Henry some years back.'

Andy heard a wagon rattling over the cold earth beyond the trees and walked down to meet it. The driver was a sturdy woman who looked in the dawnlight to be a girl rather than a woman. He guided her among the trees to the place where Marshal Lavender was lying. She climbed down, brought a wicker bag with her and shoved Toby Gregor aside with a curt order.

'No more talking. If you want to make yourselves useful, back that horse around so's the tailgate is about where I'm standing.'

As Toby and Andy went to obey, the handsome, buxom young woman knelt beside Marshal Lavender. He stared at her. It did not seem to bother her. For a fact as handsome and solidly put-up as she was being stared at by men was probably nothing new to her.

She pulled in the little wicker basket, flipped the lid up and leaned to look at Lavender's wound and its bandaging. The marshal did not open his mouth until she rocked back on her heels looking at him from eyes the colour of old gold. 'Bad,' he said, 'eh?'

She replied curtly. 'I've seen worse wounds and they didn't even stop the shot-men from talking. Who are you?'

'U.S. deputy marshal Jeff Lavender out of Denver. Who are you?'

'Corie Satinger from the emigrant settlement down-country a ways.' Corie Satinger continued to regard Marshal Lavender for a moment before speaking again. 'We could hear the gunfire down at the settlement. It sounded like a war.'

'Ma'am, it *was* a war. If you're one of those settlement people—'

119

'Marshal, we arrived from the pass through the south mountains day before yesterday. Now then, no more talk.' She leaned and cut away Andy's bandaging, wrinkled her face and tossed it aside, then leaned forward again still holding the scissors. 'Marshal, I'm going to trim off the ragged flesh.'

It hurt but she kept his mind off that by telling him that she and her family had come from Ohio, had been on the road six months; they, their horses and wagon needed a rest, which was why they had driven to the emigrant settlement.

She pulled back with pursed lips to scowl at the wound. She dug in the little wicker basket and brought forth clean bandaging material and several bottles. Lavender watched her like a hawk, but she knew what she was doing, and she did it very well.

Near the end of her work he asked how anyone as young as she was knew about bandaging wounds. Her answer came back while her head was still lowered as she checked for fresh bleeding.

'I'm not as young as you think, Marshal, and I've been sewing people up and patching wounds worse than this one ever since I graduated from nursing school back in Ohio.' She rocked back again and this time looked stonily at him as she finished. 'Including several injured settlement-men you and those other people shot up.'

She did not smile, had not smiled since she arrived. As she arose to dust needles off her long full skirt she raised her voice slightly. 'You gentlemen—if you'll lift him onto the wagon bed we can get down where he can sleep beside a roaring fire. The wound will heal but he lost much blood. All he needs now that his resistance is low, is to continue to lie on the cold ground and catch pneumonia.'

Lavender allowed Andy and the man named Gregor to ease him into the wagon with the tailgate down. He watched the handsome woman stride down to them carrying her wicker basket. He smiled as she walked past but she did not look at him.

CHAPTER TWELVE

END OF A LONG NIGHT

The Grasshopper settlement was ablaze with lighted lamps and lanterns. When Andy Lord arrived there riding beside Corie Satinger on the spring wagon he was surprised at the number of people who were abroad.

A tall, greying man with a ruddy complexion and dignified bearing came over beside the wagon and pointed. 'That's where everyone is,

121

Corie. You have the wounded man?'

'In the back.'

The tall man looked then said, 'All right. Go over and tie up in front of the store. We'll use one of the counters in there. How bad is he?'

'Lost a lot of blood but the wound itself isn't as bad as I expected.' She looked at Andy. 'Mister Lord, this is my father, Doctor Satinger.'

Andy nodded then climbed down as Corie lined out the team in the direction of a brightly lighted building with a long hitch-rack out front. As he strode along Corie's father asked questions. Andy answered them as well as he could. Once their conversation was interrupted by raised, angry voices coming from that long lighted building the doctor had said was where most of the people were. Satinger looked, then wagged his head. 'They have factions in this settlement, Mister Lord. I think every settlement we've stopped at since leaving the east had factions. It's too bad. Most of these people have more than their share of hardships without inventing new ones.'

Andy was not especially interested in the Grasshopper settlement. He helped carry Marshal Lavender inside and helped place him belly-up atop a long, wide store-counter. He stayed until the doctor and his handsome, buxom daughter had Lavender prepared for surgery, then he strolled out into the cold

122

newday morning, listened to the sounds coming from that long building, and strolled over there.

The men who had arrived behind their constable from the town of Duryea numbered ten or twelve. They were spaced out around the big, cold room with their backs to the wall, their faces toward a troubled audience of settlement people. Some of the emigrants were indignant, some were fearful, a few sat and just listened as a large, heavy man with very dark eyes and hair, laid down the law with a big gloved fist striking a small table now and then upon which he occasionally leaned. He wore a badge and an ivory-handled sixgun, and he looked capable of culling wildcats. On top of that, he was very angry.

'We have nine names,' he bellowed at the uneasy crowd. 'I'm going to call them off and they better stand up.'

A bearded man dressed like a freighter called a question. 'And if they stand up, then what?'

'I'm going to take them back to Duryea when we leave and hold them for trial whether they stand up or not!'

The big bearded man with the checkered shirt and red suspenders asked another question. 'Tried for what? An' what authority you got up here anyway?'

The dark-eyed big lawman looked steadily at his questioner. 'Horse stealing to start with, fightin' the law for another, and I'll think of

123

other charges ... What is your name?'

The bearded man did not respond until someone nudged him. Seven carbines were pointing at him from around the outer wall of the room. He cleared his throat before answering. 'My name is Wesley Trent. I haul freight into this town and that's all. I don't live here and I only get up here maybe once every couple of months. I drove in yesterday, and I expect to drive out today after I unload over at the general store.'

It seemed to Andy to be a straightforward answer. It must have seemed the same to the angry lawman from Duryea because he ignored the freighter and picked up a scrap of paper from which he began reading names.

No one stood up and there were perhaps as many as forty people in the room. The lawman paused before finishing with the names, eyed the audience, wagged his head then resumed reading. When he said, 'Ambrose and Evan Kamp,' Andy ranged a look out over the crowd. Still no one stood up. The lawman finished reading off names and afterwards remained silent. One man was on his feet. Andy thought he recognised him but was not certain. The dark-eyed lawman asked the man his name. He got a dry answer. 'Jed Carter.'

The lawman looked at his list then nodded and pointed. 'Go over by the door, Mister Carter ... Anyone else want to stand up?'

124

Evidently no one did because those who were sitting down remained that way.

Andy slipped out past two armed possemen, stepped down into the dirt of the roadway, glanced toward the general store where several lamps had been clustered in one place, then he started walking. Somewhere around here he had a horse but a half mile or so was not much of a hike.

There was a light burning inside the way-station which was visible all the way over to the settlement. Andy wondered why no one had blown it out, now that morning had arrived. The answer became evident when he swung open the heavy front door. The way-station had been abandoned. There were dying coals in the fireplace and the lighted lamp, which he blew out, and there were dishes on a table where a half-eaten meal suggested that flight had been precipitous.

He went through the building and out the rear door in the direction of the holding corrals. There were a number of harness horses but no saddle animals, and evidently because at this time of day someone usually fed them, all the horses stood like statues watching Andy.

He looked in the harness room. All the harness was on pegs but there were no saddles. He called Ezra's name several times with little hope of being answered, then strode back to the main building and made a closer inspection.

The leave-taking had been so swift that a number of drawers which had been yanked out still contained personal clothing and trinkets.

He went to the bar, poured himself a straight jolt and downed it. Charley Kinnon would have a fit, meanwhile Charley would have to find someone else to man the way-station.

Andy still had not believed Ezra was implicated even after meeting one of his sons over near the corrals. Now he had no choice but to believe Ezra had been as involved in rustling as his boys had been. It was a blow, not entirely because he had not been convinced Ezra would get involved with something like this, but because it proved his own judgement of Ezra Kamp had been wrong.

He returned to the front yard. Over at the emigrant settlement there was considerable activity. Except for Marshal Lavender he did not really care very much what was done over there. Henry Garth and his possemen could empty the whole damned settlement for all he cared, and take everyone down to Duryea to be tried as outlaws.

He leaned on a pole tie-rack watching the activity across the road and southward. It seemed that the possemen were rigging out animals for their prisoners to ride. He thought of his own horse and with a sigh shoved up off the rack and started walking toward the noise and activity.

When he came walking toward the settlement several mounted men loped out to look him over. One of them was the short, bearded man who had introduced himself as Toby Gregor. He sat his saddle scowling even after he recognised Andy, and when they were close Gregor jabbed the air with a gloved finger and said, 'Who is over there?'

'No one. Not a damned soul,' Andy replied.

Gregor put a sulphurous stare in the direction of the way-station and jerked his head. He and his companions loped across the intervening distance to make their own search leaving Andy to continue on into the emigrant town.

The noise was considerable as women tried to interfere with possemen who were shoving men toward the saddled horses. Constable Garth was already astride, Winchester balanced across his lap. Like a general of troops he missed nothing and occasionally shouted an order to someone.

That tall, thick man who had gone for the wagon to be used in carrying Jeff Lavender to the store eased up beside Andy and said, 'About half the bastards got away.'

Andy nodded. More of them should have if they'd had the sense God had given a goose. He watched some of the settlement-men being shoved and boosted atop horses by grimly dogged and silent possemen. The tall, thick man said, 'Henry wanted to burn the place. Your friend in the general store talked him out

127

of it.'

Andy looked at the tall man. 'You gents would do better to try and find the ones that got away.' He gestured toward the roiled people. 'You already got about twice as many men on horses as there were out there in the timber.'

He left the tall man, pushed through crowds of moving agitated people and stamped up onto the porch of the general store where those clustered lamps were still burning, but now their brilliance was being noticeably diluted by the spread of daylight.

There were five or six people he had never seen before in the store, looking and acting numb although they raised eyes as Andy entered. One man, nearly bald with shiny rimless glasses and a pale skin, as though he rarely got out into the sun, straightened up from behind a counter and jerked a thumb in the direction of a far door. Andy nodded and strode back there. The people watched from the centre of the room as he pushed inside and closed the door after himself. As soon as it was closed that bald man with the shiny eye-glasses said, 'I know that one. He drives stage for Deadwood Company. I've ridden with him many times.'

If that had any significance to his listeners they gave no sign of it, they were listening to the noise out front.

The room Andy had entered was part

storeroom, part boar's nest. Someone lived here, perhaps not full time but there was a cot, a little pot-bellied cook-stove and along with some hanging cooking utensils, there was also a very untidy old rolltop desk. Apparently the man who owned the store worked late in here, and if he worked too late, he also bedded down here.

But now the man occupying the cot was Marshal Lavender. He gazed at Andy without speaking or moving. Beside his cot seated upon a three-legged stool was the handsome, buxom young woman Corie Satinger. She too glanced up at Andy Lord.

Lavender did not look very good. Andy went upon the opposite side of the cot from the beautiful woman and leaned down a little to explain that the Kamps were gone. Lavender's sunken eyes glowed briefly with an expression of tired triumph and he softly said, 'I told you, Andy.'

'Yeah, you did, Marshal,' he replied and raised his eyes to the beautiful woman. 'You fixed him up?'

She nodded, gazed at Andy for a moment, then arose gesturing with her head for him to follow her. He did, and Jeff Lavender watched them both as they stepped past his doorway where he could not hear what was being said.

Andy felt worried as the handsome woman squared around on him looking solemn. 'My father closed the wound and stitched it, Mister Lord.'

Andy waited for whatever else she had to say. It was a very short wait.

'Where there is considerable loss of blood, Mister Lord, it is almost impossible to tell whether or not there has been too great a loss. Do you understand?'

Andy nodded. 'I think so. You're saying that you can't tell whether he lost so much that he'll die no matter what's done for him.'

'Yes, that's about it.'

'How long before you can tell, Miss Satinger?'

'By tomorrow without doubt. Maybe this evening. My father said he didn't think there's been too great a loss . . . I'd like to be able to tell you that I feel the same way, but I don't. I'm sorry.'

He nodded at her. 'Is he the only injured one?'

'Heavens no. One man has concussion from a fractured skull, there are two with bullet injuries, and one man has a broken ankle from his horse panicking and falling with him. There are others too, but with only bad bruises and sprains.'

She smiled ruefully up at him. It was the first time she had smiled since they had met. The smile made her look six or seven years younger.

'Several settlement-men went out with a

130

wagon to bring in the fatalities for burial . . . It's been a very hectic time around here since we drove in.' She made no move to walk away although they had exhausted the main topic, which was Marshal Lavender. 'Did that constable from some other town really have the authority to arrest people here in Grasshopper and take them somewhere else to be tried?'

Andy was on uncertain ground but he answered anyway. 'One of the settlement people, a man named Flander, bushwhacked our constable from up at Deadwood—the next town you'll pass going north. Ma'am, to my knowledge there's no other lawman around except for Mister Lavender and he isn't in shape to do what the law officer from Duryea did. That may not be exactly a good answer, Miss Satinger, but I think that's about the way folks think it ought to be handled. The alternative is to leave 'em here until someone from our area can come get 'em and if we wait that long there won't be anyone left down here to arrest.'

'Someone said a man who worked for your stage company was the brains and ringleader of the cattle and horse stealing organisation.'

Andy's eyes drifted away and back before he answered. 'Yeah. Ezra Kamp. He had charge of that way-station you can see from out front. I don't know about being ringleader though.'

As Andy said this he was thinking of how

131

cleverly old Ezra had managed to convince him that he did not like the settlement people and went over to the settlement only as a last resort. Ezra was an old scoundrel, there was no other way to describe him, but he did not mention this to the handsome woman. Instead, he said, 'He and his woman and two sons left in a big hurry, most likely last night even before the fighting ended. I met one of them in the timber and left him tied. He was gone the next time I passed that area. My guess is that he raced for home to warn his paw. Anyway they are gone.' He smiled slightly at her. 'They'll get caught. I got no idea where or when but I've seen it happen many times—folks run from something and it always usually catches up the minute they set down to rest.'

She was interested in him and it showed as she said, 'Marshal Lavender told us you were the best man in a fight he'd ever had with him.'

Andy laughed and looked away. 'I guess he didn't know how scairt I was.' He looked down at her again. 'Anything I can do for him?'

'No. Just wait. We'll keep him warm and comfortable and fed.'

He left her, went back over to the big building where Constable Garth had laid down the law—his law anyway—to the settlement people, but except for an old man with an old dog sitting where sunlight reached them, the place was all but deserted. The old man had shrewd, faded blue eyes and he did not stop stroking his old dog's head as he eyed Andy Lord and said, 'Hell of a tussle, warn't it? I'll tell you for a fact, mister, this will be the end of Grasshopper.'

Andy leaned in sunshine eyeing the older man. 'Naw,' he said in dissent. 'Not the end of it. Maybe the end of folks using it for stealing livestock, but there are good buildings here, good feed and water. It's close to the emigrant trails, got plenty of timber nearby.'

The old man continued to stroke his old dog. The animal settled at his feet and closed its eyes. 'Hope you're right,' he said. 'My name's Buffler Thompson. Me'n another feller—called Mandan Phillips—started this place as a tradin' post fifteen years ago when we got too old for doin' much. It prospered, mostly at first from tradin' then the emigrants commenced comin' through, trappin' and huntin' give out, and I used to tell Mandan—he's been dead a while now—I used to say Mandan, if we could jus' get that confounded stage company up in Deadwood to let us have a way-station here in town . . . but they went and put up that ugly log thing up yonder.'

Andy was interested. 'Did you ever talk to someone from the company?'

'Well, we was goin' to, but then old Mandan got sick and by the time he cashed in they was haulin' logs over there.'

'Mister Thompson, if you had the way-station over here who would man it?'

Old Buffalo Thompson smiled expansively showing healthy but toothless gums. 'That wouldn't be no problem at all. There's been a dozen young bucks livin' in Grasshopper for a long time that'd jump at the chance not to have to work out.'

Andy left the old man and his dog to go in search of his horse. He found it, along with about a half dozen other unclaimed saddle animals in a large corral at the lower end of Grasshopper. There were saddles, blankets and bridles strung out along a pine pole, evidently placed there in the hope that someone would come along and claim them.

Andy was not quite ready to ride so he foraged for a hay pile and pitched feed to the animals, then he went in search of something to eat, and after that requirement had been taken care of by a sullen older woman who operated a little hole-in-the-wall cafe he returned to the general store where things seemed to be returning to normal. He bought a cake of lye soap from the balding man with the shiny eye-glasses, asked directions to the bath-house and was told how to reach the creek behind town out through the timber, and hiked out there to bathe, and to afterwards lie in hot sunlight to dry off—and fell asleep.

CHAPTER THIRTEEN

A SURPRISE!

The sun was high when he awakened, it was hot even among the big trees and up along the creek. He opened his eyes, waited a moment, then heard a voice and sprang up to lunge for his britches and shirt.

He hadn't pulled on his boots before a large, shaggy dog walked up across the creek and eyed him without wagging his tail or barking. He just stood there watching the two-legged creature struggle into its boots, neither hostile nor friendly. Andy stamped his boots a couple of times then spoke to the dog. His reply was a faint, tentative wag of the animal's tail, and that tickled the man so he laughed. Now, the dog decided the man was not unfriendly, and plunged across the creek, tail wagging furiously.

Andy leaned to scratch the dog's back. The dog stood looking up into his face and an amused voice said, 'Mister Cedric said you might be over here.' It was the buxom, handsome woman. She forded the creek in a gravelly, shallow place, paused to stamp her boots then came a little closer eyeing Andy. He smiled at her and waited, because if she had been looking for him she had something to say. The big, hairy dog looked back and forth between them wagging his tail and turned away from Andy to go stand with Corie Satinger. Andy picked up his hat as she spoke again.

'Mister Lavender asked if I'd find you.'

'How is he?'

'I was evidently wrong and my father was right. He apparently had not lost as much blood as I thought. His mind is clear but he's weak and will probably remain that way for some time. How long I could only guess—but maybe for several weeks.' She moved closer and halted in fragrant fir-shade. 'There is a stagecoach in the settlement.'

Andy's eyes widened. 'Does it have a name on it?'

'Yes. It's a Deadwood stage, one of yours.'

He was puzzled. 'They never come over here.'

'Yes, so the driver told Mister Lavender, but this time someone up in Deadwood told the driver to. They heard about the fight down here and someone named Kinnon up in Deadwood sent the coach because he was told up there that you and Marshal Lavender were in the fight last night.'

Andy shrugged. How this had reached Deadwood was anyone's guess. To his knowledge no one had left the emigrant settlement heading for Deadwood, but all that

136

seemed to signify was that he had not known everything that had occurred last night.

Corie Satinger dispelled part of the mystery in her next sentence. 'Mister Kinnon heard that one of you, either the federal officer or you, got shot last night.'

Andy nodded. So that was why Charley had sent down the coach.

'And Marshal Lavender wanted me to find you so that the pair of you could be on the stage when it turns back for Deadwood.'

Andy leaned against a tree looking at her. Even last night in very poor light she had appeared very handsome and capable. This morning in filtered sunlight standing with the big dog and looking back at him, he thought she was beautiful. He did not think about her capable efficiency this time.

He asked if she thought Jeff Lavender could travel and without hesitation she shook her head. 'No. And we both told him so; my father and I both told him the jolting and jarring would almost certainly start his bleeding again.'

Andy could envisage Lavender's reaction. 'And he argued?'

An impish grin came and went across her face. 'Not exactly. He doesn't seem to be one of those bull-headed men who pound on tables and swear.'

Andy could accept that. His impression of Marshal Lavender from the beginning of their association was that the federal deputy was one of those shrewd, sly individuals who got their way without being strident about it.

'But in his easy way he was adamant and he wants you on the stage with him.'

'Well, I have a saddle horse.'

'You could ride beside the coach couldn't you?'

He eyed her. 'One minute you say he shouldn't be moved, in the next breath you seem willing for him to make the trip.'

She made a little slow smile. 'He shouldn't. He knows it. He is polite. He listened to everything my father said, and to what I had to say, and after a moment he told us he would watch the bandages and he'd tell the driver to be very careful, but he had to go back up there today.'

Corie Satinger threw up her hands and laughed. 'How do you make that kind of a person do what's best for them?'

Andy did not know. Nor did he know what the big rush was; they had accomplished what they had come down here to do, and even though things had gotten out of hand when the possemen from Duryea arrived, the end result had been what he would be willing to accept: They had broken up the rustling ring, had recovered the horses stolen from that cow outfit north of Deadwood, and had vindicated Lavender's doubts about the Kamps. Also, they

138

had killed several of the thieves and had put the fear of God into the settlement people. There was very little left to do, except rest before starting north, and to eventually compile the facts about the rustlers who had escaped, including Ezra and his boys, to be printed onto wanted dodgers.

'Did he say what the hurry was?' he asked, and the handsome woman shook her head.

The dog returned to Andy's side for more back-scratching. As he leaned to comply the beautiful woman said, 'There is a better way, Mister Lord. We can make him comfortable in our wagon, put layers of cloth under him so he will not be jarred nor shaken, and my mother is a very good teamster. We can take him up to Deadwood.'

He looked at her. 'Why should you do it?'

'Because if we don't I'm afraid he will not be alive when he reaches your town.'

'You folks have other things to do rather than . . .'

'We have nothing to do, Mister Lord. We were going to head north anyway.'

He thought about that. 'North is a lot of country. You have a place in mind?'

'No, not really, but we'll have to settle down soon. But that's not the point is it? We will be glad to deliver him up in Deadwood alive. The other way, regardless of how careful the driver is, I've ridden on my share of stages . . .' She

139

looked at him without completing her sentence, expecting him to understand.

He did. No one would have understood better; he was a driver, he knew how uncomfortable even the best stagecoach was. But it seemed to be an awful imposition and he would have taken that up again but the handsome woman silenced him very effectively.

'I'm sure you would agree that our way is best for your friend.' She offered Andy no opportunity to agree or disagree. 'We did not discuss it with Marshal Lavender. In fact neither of us even thought of it until after he'd told us that he was going to go up to Deadwood come hell or high water ... I told you my reason for searching for you, Mister Lord—now I'll tell you my personal reason: We want you to convince Marshal Lavender to let the Deadwood coach go back empty and let us take him up there in our outfit. It will be slower but I think you've heard the saying that it would be better to be late in Deadwood than early in hell?'

He laughed at her, in an era when entire generations of women went their whole lifetimes without saying the word 'hell' at least out loud among people they either did not know well or did not know at all, she was refreshing. He already knew she could be peremptory, he had encountered that last night.

Her eyes twinkled at his laughter but she did

140

not smile. 'Can you talk him into it?' she asked, then made a little hand-gesture as she added another sentence. 'Men! Hard as iron and twice as dense.'

He looked at her with increasing respect. Beauty, he told himself, might be its own reward, but a combination of beauty and brain offered much greater opportunities for more tangible and enduring rewards.

'Yes'm, I'll do my best.'

She looked at the towel and bar of soap in the grass. 'Did I interrupt something?'

'No. I had my bath.'

She considered him with her head slightly to one side. 'I'm sure my father will loan you a razor. Can we walk back together?'

They re-crossed the creek at its shallow place and with the dog foraging ahead started for the settlement. It was warm and fragrant among the large old trees. Andy was very conscious of her nearness. He had questions but asked none of them. In fact they said very little as they strode ahead, and when they reached the back-lots of the settlement she left him.

The place was calmer than it had been. It was also nearly deserted or at least gave that impression. Even the old red-bodied Deadwood stage standing in front of the general store had drawn no onlookers although it was the first time a Deadwood coach had come to the emigrant town.

At the general store business must have been very slack because the bald proprietor who wore shiny eye-glasses was standing on his worn wooden porch in casual conversation with that old man Andy had met previously, Buffler Thompson. The old man threw Andy a wide, friendly smile but the storekeeper limited himself to a slow and unsmiling nod.

Marshal Lavender had been sleeping. When Andy walked in the lawman turned just his eyes to see who his visitor was. 'Where you been?' he asked gruffly.

'Sluiced off at the creek and took a nap,' replied the stager as he went to one of two chairs someone had brought into the room. As he seated himself and eyed the lawman he thought Lavender looked marginally better. He certainly had a better, sharper light in his eyes.

Before Andy could speak Lavender said, 'The coach-driver was in here a while back. He's anxious to be under way. He went somewhere to see about a bait of grain for his hitch.'

Andy got comfortable as he regarded the older man. Finally he said, 'Marshal, you're not going up to Deadwood in that coach.'

Lavender's face got pink. 'You too?'

'What difference does it make whether you get up there today or next week?'

Lavender considered Andy over a moment of silence before replying. 'I'm goin' to have the same trouble with you I had with that doctor and his girl. Mister Lord, some of those men got away.'

'All right, Marshal, they got away. I'd make a guess that most of them didn't; that those riders from Duryea got the biggest part of them.'

Lavender glowered. 'Along with some innocent men. That confounded constable from that town ... I just wish I'd been able to stand on my own two feet last night when he was runnin' over everyone like a Hun.'

Andy did not pursue this topic because he did not want to have to deal with an angry federal lawman if he could avoid it. 'Marshal, you're goin' to be able to reach Deadwood, but not in one of the company's coaches.'

Lavender's eyebrows shot up. 'You got a flyin' machine?'

Andy ignored that. 'The Satingers will take you up there in their wagon.'

Lavender was surprised, then his eyes narrowed. 'Emigrant wagon?'

'Yes. They—'

'An emigrant wagon wouldn't reach Deadwood until maybe tomorrow night at the best.'

Andy sighed and tried a second time. 'I'll tell you something, Marshal. I've been driving that coach parked outside for five years and more, off and on. In your condition a ride in that thing will kill you. Take my word for it, I know what I'm talkin' about.'

Andy watched Lavender gathering his strength to argue and held up a hand. 'Marshal, you're goin' in their emigrant wagon. They'll look after you. You won't be bumped and jostled.'

Lavender's pink colour returned. He stared at Andy for a while then said, 'You're a stage-driver. That's all you are. I'm a deputy U.S. marshal.'

Andy smiled and leaned to arise from the chair. 'Mister Lavender right now I wouldn't budge if you were the President of Montana. You're goin' on their wagon. I'm not goin' to argue about it with you and I'm not goin' to try and jolly you into doing it.' Andy was standing up. He showed no anger, no hostility, just quiet, immovable resolution, and possibly Marshal Lavender recognised this, along with his own obvious inability to force things to be different. He said,

'The reason I got to get to Deadwood is because I got to write out the wanted dodgers for the men who got away. I also got to write my report to Denver. Then there's McLaughlin, the man who fixed things so you and I would come down here together. He's got to be told what all happened down here.'

Andy was at a loss about this. McLaughlin was the biggest shareholder in the company Andy worked for. He was Chairman of the
144

Board of Directors, but what that had to do with Lavender and his work Andy could not imagine. He sounded puzzled when he said, 'McLaughlin...?'

Lavender let a moment pass before explaining. 'Do you recollect that the time you carried me down to the Grasshopper way-station you brought as light freight a little box someone said contained new JIC bits?'

Andy remembered and nodded his head.

'JIC bit like hell, Mister Lord, but what I had to figure out was whether you were in on it too.'

'In on what; what the hell are you talking about, Marshal?'

'Charles Kinnon was the man who supplied Ezra Kamp with the names and location of cow outfits for the horsethieves to raid. He knows everyone in the countryside. He's been doin' this as near as I can figure for about two years.'

Andy stared. 'Charley...?'

Lavender ignored Lord's astonishment. 'That little box with the JIC bits—well—there were for a fact five new bits in it, but they could just as easily been rocks. Any time Kinnon had to let Kamp know something fast and couldn't ride down there himself, he'd send one of you fellers even if he had to do it without either freight or passengers. The name of the outfit to be raided an' a map of how to get there and where the loose-stock was, he rolled into a little

145

wad an' put in with the other wrappings. I knew what was in that box.'

Andy stood like a statue gazing at the man in the bed. Charley Kinnon the mastermind of a band of horsethieves? He finally said, 'That sounds crazy. I've worked for Charley—'

'Yeah. So did Kamp. So did some of the yardmen. That's the main reason I wanted to fetch you down here with me. I wanted you right there at that corral with the other horsethieves. I wanted to prove that you were one of them—or that you weren't.' Lavender paused to clear his throat before saying any more. 'I didn't expect to get the answer quite the way I got it—with just you an' me against the whole herd of them—but I'll tell you flat out, I was glad you weren't one of them.'

'What the hell ever made you think I was?'

'You brought that little box down to Kamp and I know for a fact you've brought other little boxes down to him. Y'see, Mister Lord, when Mister McLaughlin contacted the marshal's office, he had already got a man hired on by Kinnon as one of the hostlers. That man was a Pinkerton detective.'

Andy looked around and sat down again. He shoved back his hat and ran a callused hand over his scratchy jaw. The sound reminded him what Corie Satinger had said about him needing a shave.

When he had sorted it all out he said, 'You're

146

still going back in an emigrant wagon. Give me one good reason why you shouldn't go back that way?'

'Damn it, that's what I've been tryin' to get through your thick skull—because Mister McLaughlin's got to know what I found out down here so's he can jump Kinnon and whoever was workin' for him at the company yard.'

Andy turned this over in his mind and came up with what seemed to him to be a good solution, so he arose from the chair again as he said, 'I'll leave now on horseback. I can be in Deadwood right after supper. I'll look up Mister McLaughlin and tell him everything we been talkin' about. I'll even help him get Charley and whoever's been working for him at the corralyard—but you're going back in the emigrant outfit.'

He left the room quickly. Even so as he was closing the door he could hear Marshal Lavender's gravelly profanity.

Now there were a few customers in the store and as Andy passed them, and the proprietor, on his way out into the roadway to hunt for the driver of the coach parked in front, he received a more congenial nod from the man with the shiny eye-glasses.

The driver, as Charley had promised, was Buster Munzer. He was sitting by himself in shade upon the far side of the settlement's only

147

road eating peaches from a tin using a long-bladed bootknife as a fork.

When Andy approached, Munzer, who was a freckled, thick man with a big smile, began wagging his head. He speared half a peach as he said, 'When Charley said I was to take your south run this morning I thought you was maybe sick or hurt . . . Want some peaches? . . . I never in this world would have imagined what I'd be drivin' into. Ezra's gone from the way-station along with his boys and his woman, and the best saddle animals, an' over here you and some other feller, plus some stockmen from down around Duryea nearly wiped out the population of this town. Andy, how the hell did you get caught up in all this—how did you happen to even be over here? Nobody from the corralyard ever come over here before. Charley told me a dozen times these folks are the dregs of eastern cities and we should keep plumb away from them.'

Andy sat down beside Munzer, declined the offer of a peach, and without explaining anything, said, 'You can head back when you're through eating. Alone.'

The freckled man turned his face. 'Not alone. I'm supposed to take that wounded feller back with me.'

'Alone, Buster. The wounded feller isn't going back with you.'

'Yeah? Then what am I supposed to tell

148

Charley?'

'Nothing. I'm going to saddle up and start back directly. I'll talk to Charley when I get up there.'

Munzer chewed and swallowed the last of his tinned peaches and carefully shoved the empty container under some rocks as he said, 'Andy, just what the hell is going on?'

Andy stood up, slapped Munzer lightly on the shoulder as he said, 'When you get back to Deadwood, if Mister McLaughlin's at the office with Charley, wait outside and when he comes out tell him where no one else can hear you—especially not Charley—that I'll be along directly to talk to him. All right, Buster?'

The freckled man looked baffled as he also arose. 'Andy . . . ?'

'Maybe next week when we can get together at the saloon I'll tell you the whole story. Remember, Buster, not a word to McLaughlin where Charley can hear you.'

Buster Munzer stood in the shade watching Andy as he walked away.

CHAPTER FOURTEEN

A DAY OF SUNSHINE

He moved with the quickness of someone with a mission, which in fact he was. He did not see the tall, greying man who was watching until he turned to lead his horse out into the back alley, then the greying man smiled slightly. It was Corie's father, the medical practitioner. Andy halted as the older man strolled toward him from in front of the harness room, and while Andy did not feel he owed him an explanation he felt obligated to his daughter, so he said, 'Marshal Lavender will ride up to Deadwood in your wagon. He's not exactly happy about that, but I've sent the stagecoach back so unless he wants to crawl, your wagon is the only way he can get up there.'

The greying man nodded without speaking.

'And ... If you were to tell your daughter that's the arrangement ... and that I'm heading for Deadwood now so I'll be up there when you folks arrive tomorrow.' Andy paused. 'I'll explain when we meet in Deadwood. Something came up...'

The doctor's expression had not changed and it did not change now as he replied. 'She thought you might want to ride up beside our wagon. I'll tell her.'

Andy smiled. 'I'm obliged. Now I'd better be getting along.'

The physician walked out back and watched Andy Lord ride northward at a steady walk. When Andy boosted his horse over into a lope beyond the settlement the greying man turned thoughtfully back up through the barn.

There was heat so Andy alternated between walking and loping. Up ahead where a faint showing of dust marred the otherwise perfect visibility he occasionally caught a reflection of red colouring. Buster must have left the settlement about the time Andy had left him. He would arrive in Deadwood first but Andy would not be very far behind.

As he passed the vacated Grasshopper way-station he thought of Ezra Kamp and the marshal's mentioning of Andy's incorrect judgement. With a bleak expression he continued ahead. It was not the only time in his life he had misjudged an individual, and probably would not be the last, but until enough time had passed for him to be able to view this philosophically he was bitter.

The horse was rested and had been well fed. He was perfectly willing to make haste, so willing in fact that Andy had to restrain him for about half the distance. After that the horse willingly slogged along.

They had Deadwood in sight—its lights in

sight—a couple of hours after nightfall. No one saw Andy go up the back alley. He did not ride up to the corralyard but left his horse among the public corrals and after making sure that it had water and feed, he stood in darkness eyeing the lights along Main Street. The stage company's office was lighted, so was the corralyard where men were finishing up taking care of Buster Munzer's coach.

Andy went over to the cafe, ate, drank hot coffee, then strolled up to the saloon and looked over the top of the spindle doors prior to entering. It was fortunate that he had because although there was no sign of Andrew McLaughlin, Charley Kinnon was at the bar in casual conversation with a rancher.

Andy turned, considered the lighted office across the road and hiked over there. It turned out to be a good guess. Andrew McLaughlin was seated at Charley's desk laboriously writing something, and when Lord walked in the sandy-haired, square-jawed older man looked up squinting against the glare of his writing lamp.

He leaned back, tossed down the pen and said, 'All right; I've been killing time waiting for you. Munzer nailed me out back in the corralyard. Sit down, Mister Lord.'

Andy sat, shoved out his legs, tipped back his hat and quietly began talking. McLaughlin did not interrupt, he watched Lord and he listened.

152

When Andy finished McLaughlin leaned forward in the old chair and spoke bluntly. 'I'm glad Jeff wasn't hurt worse. He and I go back a long ways.'

'So he said, Mister McLaughlin. If you care to I suppose we can wait until he arrives in town tomorrow.'

The square-jawed, hard-eyed man shook his head just once. 'No. I know all I have to know.'

'Who worked with Charley out back?'

McLaughlin's reply was a question. 'Do you know a man named Russ Hagerty?'

Andy eyed McLaughlin for a moment before nodding. Hagerty was the corralyard boss. Andy had known him for years. It was a jolt. Hagerty and Andy were good friends.

McLaughlin made a bleak smile. 'I'd say from your expression it's a surprise to you.'

'It is, Mister McLaughlin. You're sure?'

The older man did not speak, he moved his head up and down.

Andy blew out a big breath. 'Is he out back in the bunkhouse?'

McLaughlin nodded again without taking his eyes off Andy.

'Charley's over at the saloon,' Andy said, 'at the bar with one of the outlying ranchers. What did you have in mind?'

'Since Marshal Lavender told you about the Pinkerton detective, I'll tell you the rest of it. He's also over at the saloon to keep an eye on

153

Charley. I'll walk over there and nod at him over the doors, then I'll come back here and you and I will go get Hagerty. Does that sound all right to you?'

Andy considered his scuffed toes. The idea of throwing down on a man who had done him favours over the years was not all right, but nothing that had happened to him over the last couple of days was all right. He nodded, meeting the older man's gaze, and McLaughlin arose to pull a coat from the back of his chair. Sitting down, Andy had been unable to see the shellbelt and holstered Colt. He eyed them now as McLaughlin shrugged into his coat. When their eyes met the older man made a small gesture of resignation. 'I've known Charley Kinnon for about seven or eight years. I'm no more delighted about what I have to do than you are.' McLaughlin held up a key. 'To the jailhouse. I'll lock Charley in then I'll be back. There's fresh coffee.'

Andy did not move even after McLaughlin had left. He felt tired again. Someone grasped the latch of the rear door, which opened into the office from the corralyard. Andy raised his eyes as sure as he had ever been of anything who was going to walk in, and he was right.

Russ Hagerty was a large, hearty man with a wide smile and grey at the temples. He had been corralyard boss since before Andy Lord arrived in Deadwood. He had done Andy

154

favours, they had played poker and had a few drinks together.

Hagerty seemed surprised to see Andy sitting there, but he showed a quick, warm smile as he shoved the door closed at his back and walked toward the stove and the coffee pot. 'Buster came in a couple of hours ago. He didn't say anything about you coming along ... Coffee, Andy?'

'No thanks.' Lord watched the other man seat himself near the stove holding his coffee cup. 'Cold out,' Hagerty said, and with the cup almost to his lips, eyed Andy over the rim, then continued to hold the cup as he said, 'What's wrong?'

Andy said, 'You carryin' a gun, Russ?'

The cup slid down a few inches. 'No. Why?'

Andy let his breath out slowly eyeing his friend. 'You damned fool,' he said, and this time Hagerty leaned to place the untouched cup on the edge of Kinnon's desk.

'Russ, what in the hell did you do it for?'

'... Do what?'

'Work with Charley lining up livestock raids on the outlying cow outfits.'

Hagerty parted his lips to speak, probably to make a blustery denial, but the look on Lord's face held him silent for a moment.

'We're going down to the jailhouse, Russ,' stated Andy, leaning to arise.

Hagerty finally found his tongue. 'You're

talkin' through your hat.'

Standing up Andy slowly shook his head. 'No. Ezra got away and the gang at the Grasshopper settlement who were doing the raiding are in custody down at Duryea. Russ, did you hire a man a couple of months back who was new to the country?'

'Yes, I guess you mean—'

'That was a hell of a mistake, Russ. He is a Pinkerton detective.' At the yardboss's blank look Andy also said, 'I don't know the details of how they figured out you and Charley were in this mess along with Ezra and those settlement men, but they did. Mister McLaughlin and the Pinkerton man are picking Charley up now over at the saloon. Come along, let's take a little walk.'

Hagerty arose, the colour had left his normally ruddy face. 'Andy?'

'What.'

'Just the two of us know I walked in that back door.'

Andy shook his head and went to the roadway door to hold it open as he jerked his head for the yardboss to precede him out into the night. Hagerty did not move so Andy said, 'I don't like this one damned bit better than you do. Of all the men in this town you're about the last one I want to lock up.'

'Well, then, Andy...'

'Come on, Russ. Walk ahead of me and don't

reach in a pocket and don't turn around. *Move!*'

There were lights at the jailhouse which meant McLaughlin and the Pinkerton man were already down there with Charley Kinnon. Andy marched Hagerty down there without a word passing between them. When he shoved in out of the night lamplight temporarily bothered him, but the two men who turned as the door had opened did not have this problem. The man standing with McLaughlin knew Andy and nodded. Andy nodded back. It made a difference knowing a man who had shared the bunkhouse with him was not just a corralyard hostler.

McLaughlin was staring at Hagerty, his mouth flat and bloodless. With a brusque gesture he told the Pinkerton detective to take their second prisoner down into the cell room and lock him up.

When McLaughlin and Lord were alone the older man said, 'Andy, I'm sorry. You likely don't believe that. You likely think of McLaughlin as a company executive who has been coming down here lately to nose around. Well, that would be right. But now you know why.' McLaughlin stepped toward the dusty desk Lew Brant had used and perched upon a corner of it eyeing Andy Lord. 'It's over. You and Jeff did a hell of a job ... Andy, the company has got to have someone it can trust and who knows the equipment and the routes.'

McLaughlin paused before adding: 'The pay as Deadwood supervisor for the company would be about three times what you are getting as a driver. And you'd be in town in your own bed every night. No more rolling out when there's two feet of snow on the ground.' McLaughlin paused again. 'If you'll take the job I'll be relieved as hell ... Well?'

Andy was turning toward the door as he said, 'Let me sleep on it, Mister McLaughlin.'

The older man gave one of those brusque nods of the head which appeared to be one of his characteristics. 'All right. But I'm leaving tomorrow afternoon.'

'I'll have an answer for you by then. Good night, sir.'

Andy went up to the roominghouse, bedded down and did not even hear noise until the sun was high the following morning. He had not slept-in like that in years. He went out back to clean up and shave, then he went over to the cafe for breakfast, only the proprietor called it 'dinner'.

He emerged from the cafe to look northward—and saw an emigrant wagon up in front of Doctor Brady's place. Hell, the Satingers must have driven all night. He walked up there.

As he turned in at the little picket gate a voice spoke softly and he turned. Corie was sitting on the high seat of the big wagon. He walked over to lean on the forewheel and smile upwards.

Her eyes twinkled. 'You shaved.'

His smile widened. 'You drove all night?'

'Yes. My mother and father spelled each other off. I remained in back with the marshal.' She saw his smile fading and guessed the reason so she also said, 'He arrived in fine shape. No bleeding at all. In fact he slept most of the way. When he slept so did I.' She glanced at the patiently-standing big horses and leaned to loop the lines and set the brakes, then offered him her hand as she started to climb down. When she was on the plankwalk she looked up at him. 'This is a very attractive town, trees, little garden patches, painted storefronts . . . I like it. Do you like it?'

He nodded. 'I liked it the first time I saw it about ten years ago.' She continued to look at him. 'Of course if you're going north . . .'

'Yes? If I am going north—what?'

He could feel the heat in his cheeks because her eyes did not leave his face. 'Well . . . if you are goin' on north, why then I expect I'll just sort of follow . . . until you tell me not to.'

Her steady large eyes misted slightly and her lips lifted slightly at the corners in a soft little smile. 'I wouldn't tell you not to . . . but maybe I won't go north. Maybe none of us will because my father and the doctor in there, Mister Brady, hit it off like long-lost brothers. Mister Brady wants my father to stay on. Andy?'

'Yes'm.'

'I'm Corie, not yes'm.'

'Yes, Corie.'

Her eyes finally sprang away from his face and roamed the far distances north of Deadwood, and she coloured slightly. She hung fire so long he finally had to prompt her.

'Yes, Corie.'

'Would you show me the town?'

He hooked his arm into her arm and turned with her walking slowly in warm mid-day sunlight down toward the centre of Deadwood, and when he reached the corralyard a stocky man with sandy hair, unemotional grey eyes and an expression that was quite different than the expressions he had showed last night, smiled at them.

Andy stopped and introduced Corie Satinger to Andrew McLaughlin. His look of approval was accented by a smile. Then he said, 'Andy...?'

'I'll take the job, Mister McLaughlin.'

The older man's gaze drifted back to Corie Satinger. 'Son,' he said in a pleasant gruff voice, 'I don't blame you one bit.' He pushed out a large, square hand. Andy gripped it, nodded and with their arms still hooked began leading Corie down toward the lower end of town.

When they were half-way along she looked up at him. 'What did he mean?'

'He offered me the job of company supervisor here in Deadwood last night. I told him I'd think about it.' Andy smiled at her. 'It means I won't be driving, I'll run the office and yard from here in town. I'll be able to keep fairly regular hours.'

She said no more. They reached the south end of Deadwood, stood down there for a moment gazing southward where so many things had happened, including finding one another, then she gave his hand a hard squeeze and they turned back, crossed to the opposite plankwalk and resumed their stroll.

She asked if he believed in pre-destination and he had to think before answering. 'Never thought about it. Do you?'

She was gazing straight ahead when she replied. 'I haven't thought much about it either ... Right now I'm thinking about it.'

He squeezed her hand and they continued to walk.

Photoset, printed and bound in Great Britain by REDWOOD PRESS LIMITED, Melksham, Wiltshire